THE SPIRIT OF TH

C000136378

THE CASE
OF THE
FOUR FINGERS

LIZ HEDGECOCK

WHITE
RHINO
BOOKS

ISBN-13: 979-8360855729

For the team behind
the Heritage Open Days initiative,
without whom this story would not exist!

CHAPTER 1

'Guess what, Steph?'

My desk creaked. I looked up from the report I was reading to see Huw Jones half-sitting on it and grinning at me.

'What, Huw?' I replied, trying to sound matter-of-fact and cool, though inside I was anything but. I was dying for a bit of excitement. Even new biscuits in the tin would have been something.

'It's your lucky day: Inspector Farnsworth wants to see you in his office.'

'Really?' I was already out of my seat, smoothing my hair and checking I had no traces of lunchtime's hummus and salad wrap around my mouth. A horrible thought struck me. 'Do you know what it's about?'

I racked my brain for anything I had done that might land me in trouble. My conscience was clear, as far as I knew. To be honest, I hadn't had much to do since arriving at Erskine Street police station the week before. I'd been out on the beat once with Huw, a fellow constable, during which he'd pointed out every coffee shop and takeaway along the route, together with a review. The rest of the time I was glued to my desk. Sergeant Doughty had set me some reading: an email full of links to hefty reports on Liverpool and its crime statistics. When I had requested a transfer from rural Cheshire to the big city, spending my days staring at a screen wasn't exactly what I'd had in mind.

Huw continued to smile. 'You'll like this, Steph. Bit of responsibility for you.'

'Oh.' I straightened up. Whatever my previous boss, Inspector Bostock, had written about me must have been good. I mean, it wasn't that I thought she'd say anything negative. But, well, you never know.

'He'll be waiting, Steph.'

'Yes, of course. Sorry.' I checked my pocket for a notebook, then set off at a fast walk for the inspector's office, careful not to trip over my own feet.

Inspector Farnsworth was a tall, broad man who somehow managed to fade into the background, even in an office with his name on the door. I imagined that was good for shadowing people, but it made him strangely unmemorable. I was glad the meeting was in his office, as otherwise I didn't think I'd be able to pick him out of a lineup.

'Constable.' He looked at a scribbled note on his blotter. 'Stephanie, isn't it?' He smiled at me.

'That's right, sir. PC Jones said you wanted to see me.'

'Yes, Constable.' He gazed at something over my right shoulder. When I peeked round I realised it was the open door.

'Oh, sorry, sir.' I leapt up and closed it.

'Thank you, Stephanie.' He fiddled with a paperclip for a few seconds. 'We wouldn't normally do this, but in view of your exemplary record...'

'Yes, Inspector?' I was practically on the edge of my seat. I had studied the case board, I'd asked questions – without being intrusive, of course – and I was confident I knew as much as I could possibly be expected to know about any of the high-profile and juicy cases currently under investigation.

'We're putting you in charge of your own police station.'

My mouth dropped open. 'Really, sir? I mean, it's a great honour, but surely a constable couldn't possibly—'

A laugh popped out of the inspector like a cork from a bottle. 'I'm afraid I've got your hopes up, Constable. It is a police station, but . . . it's the Bridewell.'

My heart sank. The Bridewell stuck out like an old-fashioned thumb in the middle of the shiny new buildings off Prescot Street. It was still a police station, just. I'd heard other officers talk about doing a stint at the Bridewell. That seemed to involve taking a good book, a pint of milk and a supply of teabags, and whiling away a shift with perhaps one report of a lost dog or a missing wheelie bin. *Line of Duty* it was not.

A loophole presented itself to me. 'Are you sure I'm senior enough to do that, Inspector? Should managing a police station be a constable's job?'

Inspector Farnsworth shook his head regretfully. 'I'm afraid we are so chock-a-block with cases that I can't possibly spare anybody else.'

I tried to hide the sting of that remark. Was I the worst possible option for proper police work? What had Inspector Bostock written about me in her report?

I exhaled slowly, rather than heaving the sigh that was struggling to escape. 'When would you like me to start, sir?'

The inspector turned to his computer, pressed a couple of keys and peered at the screen. 'Sam Davies is there at the moment, and we could use her on the Kensington off-licence break-in. Can you get your things together and head down now, Stephanie?' He gave me an encouraging, you-can-do-it kind of smile.

'Yes, sir.' I got up, finding it a struggle as my heart had sunk so low, and made a swift exit.

'Bridewell duty, eh, Steph? You've arrived.' Tasha

Saunders gave me a gentle punch on the arm. I was slightly in awe of her, mostly because she seemed entirely too glamorous to be a police constable. She looked more as if she was dressed as one for a photoshoot.

'Um, thanks. If you want to swap—'

'You're OK.' She grinned at me, then fished in her bag and handed me a Snickers. 'Emergency chocolate. You can thank me later.' But even unexpected chocolate couldn't cheer me up.

I thought of something I'd forgotten to ask Inspector Farnsworth. 'How long does it normally last, Bridewell duty?'

Tasha tossed her auburn mane. 'Till someone comes to replace you, generally.'

I pinched the bridge of my nose. 'I wish I hadn't asked. Seriously, is there nothing to do there?'

'Not a thing. Sergeant Doughty tried getting people to take a laptop down and type up statements, but the laptop kept going funny. Static on the screen, wouldn't save the document, that sort of thing. Get yourself a few magazines on the way. Catch up on some sleep, if you like. Maybe grab a snack, too.'

I forced a smile. 'Maybe I'll get a takeaway delivered from one of Huw's recommendations.'

A tiny frown creased the skin between Tasha's arched eyebrows. 'Nowhere delivers to the Bridewell.'

I made a face. 'This gets better and better.' And so,

after thumping my copy of *Blackstone's Police Operational Handbook* and the latest issue of *Police* magazine into my bag, putting on my hat, clattering round the kitchenette gathering supplies, and generally making it clear that I wasn't happy about my new work location, I set off for the Bridewell.

CHAPTER 2

Despite using my phone as a satnav, it took me some time to find my way into the Bridewell.

I arrived first at a metal gate which was locked, with the doorbell hanging from a wire. I stared up at the building, an uncompromising square block of red brick and yellow stone, with large many-paned windows. It was in surprisingly good condition. However, I hadn't seen inside, and when I'd overheard the others talking about it, the word I recalled was 'dump'. I sighed, and kept walking in search of another door.

I found a more promising door, but when I tried it it was locked, and it looked thick enough to drown out a knock. *Maybe it's a sign that I shouldn't be here. Maybe I should go back to the station and say I couldn't find my way in.* But the thought of the sniggers from the team, and the ribbing I would receive, possibly for the rest of my career there, made me keep going.

At last I found a door on the third side of the building which had been left ajar. I knocked, then pushed it open.

The building seemed solid, with municipal brown tiles halfway up the walls and a wooden floor like a school hall, but bits of wood and broken furniture were propped against the walls, along with a box of light fittings.

'Hello?' I called. My voice echoed in the curtainless, carpetless space.

Eventually, the reply 'Coming' floated from above. I glanced up the staircase, which looked as if it was made of concrete – was that even possible? – with the metal banister painted a surprising bright blue. At the bottom was a sign, white lettering on dark grey. A hand pointed upwards, next to the words *DETECTIVE OFFICE*.

A few seconds later, Sam Davies's head appeared above the balustrade at the top. 'Are you taking over?' she asked.

I briefly considered saying no, I'd come to bring her teabags and milk, but there was no point. 'Yes.'

'Thank God for that.' She practically ran downstairs. 'I was climbing the walls.' She saw my expression and her grin faded. 'You'll be fine. This is new to you. It's just that I've done a lot of shifts here. There's only so many shopping lists you can make and magazines you can read. No wi-fi, you see. Anyway, it won't be for long.'

'I'm glad you're so sure,' I said.

'It won't be: they're selling it to developers in a couple of weeks. It's going to be luxury flats.' I looked doubtfully around me and she giggled. 'I guess they'll knock it down. Someone's already started taking anything of value out.' She glanced at the box of light fittings.

I felt a pang of something – sorrow? regret? – but it was quickly replaced first by relief that this would last two weeks at most, then horror that I might spend two whole weeks cooling my heels, with no chance of anything interesting happening.

'Want me to give you a quick tour?' asked Sam.

'Please.'

'Come on then.' She took me into a big square room, empty apart from more stacked debris, two folding chairs, and a low table beside a plug socket. On the table stood a kettle, a carton of long-life milk, half a packet of biscuits and a selection of mugs. 'If anyone comes to the station, bring them in here. Make them a brew, maybe, but you don't have to.' She led the way out to the corridor again. 'Toilets are upstairs.' She jerked a thumb at the concrete staircase. 'If you like, you can look in the detective offices. Not that there's much to see, but there's an armchair. Don't use any other staircases apart from this one –

we're not sure how safe they are.' She grinned at me. 'Want to see the cells?'

'Erm, I suppose so.'

She led me through the corridor until we came to a large, stout door. Beyond was another, smaller corridor with a row of doors on the right hand side, each with bolts and locks. 'Here we are,' said Sam, opening one. 'Step right in.'

The cell was a rectangular room with a curved ceiling, entirely clad in the sort of cream tiles that belonged in an old-fashioned toilet. At the end was an arched, barred window set high on the wall. It was surprisingly light and well-made, but completely bare. It probably hadn't been used as an actual cell for many years.

'Two-person job, this,' said Sam. 'When I joined, the old sergeant who showed me round told me they used to nip out at pub closing time, round up anyone who looked a bit bevvied, and put them in the cells to cool off. As soon as they filled the cells, they could brew up and play cards for the rest of the shift.'

I thought of the state I'd been in after going clubbing sometimes, and felt relieved that that sergeant and his colleagues hadn't been around at the time. A draught found the back of my neck, making me shiver, and I glared at the window. *About time this place came down.* As if it had heard me, the breeze intensified.

'You all right?' said Sam. 'Come on, back to the main room and make yourself a brew. I'll nip upstairs and collect my stuff.' The big square room was warmer, and I switched on the kettle. *At least there's electricity. And hopefully, a flushing toilet.*

Before the kettle had boiled Sam was back, clutching a supermarket carrier bag and a dogeared sudoku book. She reached into the carrier bag and brought out a large ring of keys. 'Big one's for the main door and you probably won't need the others. Just make sure all windows and doors are locked when you leave. This place is meant to be open eight till six, but I doubt you'll see anyone before half nine or after half five. If then, frankly. So if you want to nip out, put a note on the door. You'll find one in the letter rack thingy. See you!' And with a cheery wave of her hand, she strolled off.

I made tea, rejecting the long-life milk in favour of the pint I had brought and helping myself to a couple of ginger nuts from the pack. I sat in one of the folding chairs and looked around me while I sipped. It felt weird. Not as if the walls were closing in: more the opposite. As if the room was getting bigger and bigger. Or maybe I was getting smaller and smaller.

I stood up, slung my bag over my shoulder, and decided to check out the detective offices. First, though, I went to the front door and put up a sign, scribbled in biro on an old envelope: *PLEASE CALL*

LOUDLY FOR ATTENTION. My first idea had been to ask callers to ring my phone, but when I checked it there was no signal. *It's like going back in time,* I thought as I pushed the drawing pin into the door, in a place where it had clearly been pushed many times before. There were so many little holes in the door that it looked as if it had woodworm. Perhaps it did.

That done, I went upstairs, checked out the toilet, which appeared old-fashioned but serviceable, and stood outside the door of what was presumably a detective office. I caught myself in the act of raising my hand to knock. *You idiot, Steph. As if anyone's in there.* I opened the door and surveyed the room. *As if anyone would stay here of their own free will.*

The room was maybe ten feet square, with a yellowed net curtain at the window, a small cream-tiled fireplace (square tiles this time), and a wing-back armchair with stuffing leaking out of the seat. Beside it was a side table with a beer mat on it. The carpet was threadbare, and showed signs of where furniture had once stood. There had been two tables or desks, and maybe a cabinet against the wall. On the wall opposite the window was a noticeboard covered in green cloth with a wooden frame, empty except for a list of regulations in case of fire and three spare drawing pins, all rusty.

I wrinkled my nose. 'Home sweet home.' I put my mug on the beer mat and lowered myself carefully into the armchair.

It didn't break, but it wasn't comfortable. The springs had lost their spring some time ago, and I suspected my bottom was inches from the floor. *Oh well.* I checked my watch. Half past three, and Sam had said people didn't usually show up after half five. I could get a bit of reading in, maybe explore a few rooms and lock up at six on the dot. And tonight I could make sure I had plenty to keep me busy tomorrow. I saw the IKEA catalogue sitting on the breakfast bar in my bare, slightly grim flat, waiting for me to make decisions. My mind's eye scanned the flat. I could bring a couple of recipe books and do a proper meal plan, then shop for the week like a grown-up instead of living on microwave meals. I could bring my yoga mat, buy cheap dumbbells and do some exercise. I could even—

The chilly breeze I'd felt earlier wafted over me, bringing me back to reality.

I blinked.

Standing in front of me was a woman in her mid to late twenties, medium height and slim, with red-gold hair. My first thought was that she must have sneaked in and crept upstairs without me hearing her. 'What do you w—'

I blinked again.

She was wearing a black jacket with bright metal buttons and a calf-length skirt. It looked like an old-fashioned uniform.

Her hair was pinned up in a bun on the back of her head.

And most worryingly of all, I could see through her to the noticeboard beyond.

CHAPTER 3

I'm not sure what I said next. I think I was too stunned to hear. I heaved myself out of the chair as the ghost said, with an outraged expression, 'Wash your mouth out, young lady!' I edged round her – I couldn't bear the thought of going through her – and wrenched the door open.

'Wait!' the ghost cried. 'You can see me.'

I didn't reply. I was too busy clattering down the stairs. Two weeks on my own planning recipes and doing bicep curls was infinitely preferable to this.

'I don't mean you any harm,' said a voice that was far closer than I'd like. I turned at the bottom of the stairs and almost jumped out of my skin. She was right behind me.

'I don't care!' I snapped. 'Go and haunt somebody else. Or go back to the graveyard, or wherever you came from.'

The ghost shifted from foot to foot silently. 'I

can't.'

'What do you mean, you can't? You've got no business scaring people. No wonder no one wants to work here.'

She twisted her hands, which were clad in little white gloves. 'You're the only one who's been able to see me.'

My heart sank like a stone. 'I can't be.'

'You are. I've been invisible for a hundred years, more or less. Imagine what that feels like.'

I tried. Sometimes I felt invisible, in meetings where I made a point which went unnoticed until two minutes later a colleague said the same thing and it immediately went up on the board. 'Uh-huh.'

'What's your name?' asked the ghost. 'I'm Nora.'

'I'm – no, wait a minute. For all I know, if I give you my name you'll do something weird like possess me.'

Nora started laughing, which didn't reassure me. 'Right, that's enough,' I said. 'I agreed to come here and twiddle my thumbs, not chat to ghosts.'

'You have to help me.' Nora stretched out her hands towards me.

I took a step back. 'I absolutely do not.'

'What are you going to do about it?' Nora looked smug. 'You have to stay here, don't you? You've got orders.'

'I'll think of something,' I said, and walked down

the corridor hoping for inspiration.

'I can go anywhere you can,' said Nora. 'This is my police station too.'

'No it isn't. You're dead.'

'So I've been here longer and I know it better. I know it from the surgeon's office to the superintendent's quarters.'

'Oh, I didn't know about those,' I said. 'Where are they?' Perhaps they would be nicer than the rest of the place.

Nora pointed upwards. 'His flat's on the roof. Through the yard and up the iron stairs. Don't disturb him, he gets ever so cranky.'

'Thank you very much.' I held up my ring of keys and set off.

'That wasn't fair!' wailed Nora, trailing behind. 'You took advantage of me!'

I laughed and kept going. Soon I was climbing the stairs, which rang pleasantly. It took a while to find the key for the door, and every so often I glanced back, expecting to find Nora at my shoulder. She wasn't there. She was standing in the doorway to the yard, shading her eyes and looking cross.

'Keep up,' I called.

Nora let her hand fall. 'I can't,' she said. 'I was always nervous of horses.'

Great. A ghost who sees things that aren't there. 'What horses?'

'You can't see them?'

'There aren't any to see. Besides, didn't you have cars, even a hundred years ago?'

'Barely,' said Nora, wrinkling her freckled nose at me. 'And just because the horses weren't all here at the same time as me, that doesn't mean they aren't here now. The superintendent was, though. And if you bother him he'll probably put you on manure duty to teach you a lesson.' She folded her arms, her mouth a thin straight line.

'There isn't any manure.' My head was starting to hurt. 'Anyway, see you later.' I opened the door to the superintendent's quarters, gave the ghost a friendly wave, much as Sam had done to me, and closed and locked the door.

It was dark inside, and I switched on my phone torch as I went into the biggest room. The window was grimy, and the cast-iron fireplace was coated with a thick layer of dust. The superintendent certainly wasn't keeping up with his housekeeping duties.

I took a deep breath. 'Anyone there?' I called.

Silence.

'Are you sure?' I grinned at the lack of either sound or disquieting chills. I prowled around the flat for a bit, but it was practically bare, like the rest of the station.

An old wooden dining chair stood in the corner of the main room. I dusted it, then sat down and pulled out *Blackstone's*. I had at least two hours to kill until I could lock up and take my leave, and I intended to spend it well away from Nora. But somehow I found myself reading the same page over and over and taking nothing in.

By quarter to six I was so fidgety that I could stand it no longer. I put the book in my bag and left, locking the door behind me. I expected Nora to be where I had left her, but she'd gone. I wasn't sure whether to be relieved or worried. I sneaked down the steps and into the main station, but there was no sign of her.

I took down the notice on the door. 'I'm off,' I called.

Still nothing.

Distinctly uneasy, I shut the door, which clanged like a prison door, then locked it with the big iron key.

I tried to cheer myself with thoughts of home. *I'll make soup. I'll make soup and wrap myself in a throw on the sofa and watch interior design shows.*

All by myself.

I regarded the ring of keys in my hand. I didn't like the thought of them being in my flat. 'I'll drop these at the station,' I said, out loud. 'That way, if anyone needs to visit overnight, they can, and I can pick them up in the morning.' And I set off at a fast walk, not looking back.

***

'How was it?' said Huw, swivelling on his chair

and grinning as I came into the main office.

'Fine,' I said. Then, after a pause, 'Weird.'

'Oh yeah,' he said. 'I suppose it is.'

So it isn't just me! 'How do you mean?'

Huw looked uncomfortable. 'Kind of creepy, being alone in that morgue.'

Did that mean he'd seen ghosts, or not? 'Why do you call it a morgue?'

He shrugged. 'Turn of phrase. What I mean is that it's so boring your mind starts playing tricks on you.'

'Such as?'

His eyes narrowed. 'Are you fishing for something?'

'No, not at all,' I said, dropping the keys into my desk drawer and slamming it shut. 'Someone said no takeaways deliver to the Bridewell, and I wondered why.'

'Oh! That's 'cause some of the older residents say the place is haunted. One time this old biddy came in when I was on duty there and told me to see to the horses. She said one of them was whinnying so loud it was putting her off her knitting.' He laughed. 'I told her to stop eating cheese because it was giving her nightmares. Nightmares! Geddit?'

'Er, yeah.' I forced out a laugh. 'So no one's ever seen a ghost at the Bridewell?'

Huw's eyebrows knitted. 'You don't believe in ghosts, do you, Steph?'

'No, of course not. I just wondered. As you do.'

'Well, you can stop wondering. No one's seen any ghosts. They don't exist, and if they did they'd probably be too scared of us to show themselves.' He turned back to the file he was reading. 'Ghosts,' he said, and snorted. 'That's a good one.'

I still didn't want to head home to my chilly flat, though. I made myself a cup of tea, and for lack of anything better to do, reopened *Blackstone's*. I was halfway down the same page when I heard someone clear their throat not far away and looked up to see Inspector Farnsworth.

I jumped to my feet. 'I'm sorry, Inspector, I didn't know you were there.'

'Don't apologise, Stephanie,' said the inspector. 'Ninja skills.' He continued to stand there.

'Is there anything I can do for you, Inspector?'

He twitched. 'Oh no, nothing really. Was everything all right at the Bridewell?'

I gave him a bright smile. 'Oh yes. Very quiet. Nobody came. No people.'

'Indeed.' He rocked slightly on the balls of his feet. 'No people.'

'Why do we still keep an officer at the Bridewell, sir?' I asked. 'Surely everyone knows to come here.'

'Generally they do,' said the inspector. 'But there's a few we must keep happy until we hand over the building and it becomes someone else's problem.'

21

'Have you spent much time at the Bridewell, sir?'

'Me?' The inspector considered. 'Not as much as I'd like. It's a fascinating place. Fascinating. Yes.' He was looking past me again, but when I checked there was nothing there. 'Anyway, you'll be back at the Bridewell bright and early tomorrow morning, Stephanie, so don't let me keep you.' And with that, he wandered off.

CHAPTER 4

I ran through the corridors of the Bridewell chased by an army of ghosts, moaning gently with their arms outstretched. They weren't moving quickly, but I couldn't shake them off, however fast I ran. I tried the door into the yard: locked. I ran upstairs and tried a window: stuck. At last I found an empty room and shut myself in before the ghosts could reach me. I gripped the door handle, panting for breath, and a hand came through the door and grabbed me with an unearthly shriek…

The shriek of my alarm.

Once I had done enough deep breathing to get my heart rate down to something like normal, I hauled myself out of bed and put on my dressing gown. After spending much of yesterday evening wondering what to do, and tossing and turning in bed for a good two hours, I was glad to reach the point where I had to make a decision. I began by going into the kitchen and making tea and toast.

Does Inspector Farnsworth know about the ghost? I thought, as I got low-fat spread and strawberry jam from the fridge. *Surely he does, or he wouldn't have come over specially to ask about the Bridewell.* Then again, he hadn't mentioned the ghosts. Or anything, really. But he clearly expected me to do my duty. 'That settles it,' I said. 'I'll have to go.'

But then what? I could go to the Bridewell and cower upstairs in the superintendent's flat, or I could face Nora. Neither option was particularly attractive. But at least if I humoured Nora I would have the run of the station, such as it was, instead of being stuck in a cold room with no light or power. I looked at the clock on the wall. *Better hurry*, I thought. *All this thinking is getting in the way of my schedule.*

The station office was quiet when I went in to get the keys, which was a relief. Having decided on a course of action, the last thing I needed was to be teased about it. I grabbed the keys and took my leave.

'Off to the Bridewell?' asked the desk sergeant, as I signed out.

'That's right,' I replied.

'Give the old dump my regards.'

'Will do.'

I pondered the building as I marched along the street, kicking fallen leaves out of the way with a pleasing swish. OK, so it wasn't for modern tastes, or much use as a police station nowadays, but if it had been maintained and redecorated, it could have been quite nice. *That's why it's going to be luxury flats, Steph. Someone else has seen the potential.*

But would they knock it down and start again? And if they did, what would happen to Nora? What about the ghost horses, and any other spirits and ghouls who had made the place their home? *What happens to ghosts when their house gets knocked down? Do they go somewhere else, or do they stay put?* I imagined Nora appearing to the new tenant of a luxury flat – maybe an accountant or something in IT – and freaking them out. Or maybe they just wouldn't see her.

I looked up and flinched as I saw the sturdy door of the Bridewell. I had no recollection of the route my feet had taken. *Am I doing the right thing?*

'Will you feel bad if you don't?' said my conscience.

I huffed. *Probably. And I do wish you'd shut up.* I fished out the keys and let myself in. 'Hello?' I called.

There was no answer.

'Nora, are you there?' I waited. 'I'm making tea.' I went into the room with the kettle and settled down with a brew and *Police* magazine.

'So you're talking to me today, are you?'

I jumped half out of my seat and the magazine slid to the floor. Nora was standing in front of me, hands

25

on hips. 'Do you have to do that?'

'No, but you deserve it. You were horrid to me yesterday. You wouldn't even introduce yourself.'

I was, rather. 'I'm sorry, but you completely freaked me out. I've never seen a ghost before.'

She studied me. 'So you're not going to run away from me today, person with no name?'

'It's Steph. And no. Not unless you or something else starts being weird.'

'I'm just me.' Nora sat on the other folding chair. 'I can't speak for anyone else round here. About being weird, as you call it, I mean.'

I sipped my tea and put it on the table. 'So . . . why are you here?'

'Well, I died and now I'm stuck.'

'You died here? In the police station? What happened?' I studied Nora in my turn, but I couldn't see any marks of violence on her. Maybe someone had put arsenic in her tea. Without knowing her better, I couldn't tell if that was likely.

Nora giggled. 'Not in the station, silly! It was the Spanish flu. Not the first wave, I think it was the third. One of our, um, regular customers probably brought it in.'

'Oh, I'm sorry.'

'That's all right, you weren't to know.' She settled in the chair.

'That still doesn't explain why you're here,' I said.

I thought back to the internet searches I had done about ghosts and their habits the previous evening. 'Is it because you've got . . . unfinished business?'

'Exactly!' Nora leaned forward, blue eyes shining. 'You have no idea how long I've had to drift around watching clumsy handling of evidence and listening to vague cross-examinations. It's enough to break your heart.'

I examined Nora's uniform. There weren't any badges of rank, but what would a woman's police uniform have looked like a hundred years ago? 'So you were a police officer?'

Nora nodded.

'A female police officer? I didn't know they existed then.'

'Oh yes,' said Nora confidently. 'Edith Smith was the first, in 1915. She could arrest people and everything. We were so happy when we read about her in the newspaper. Equality at last, or something like it.' She gazed at her feet in their sensible shoes, reflecting. 'I never did get to vote.'

I dragged my mind back to school history lessons. 'So you died before 1918?'

Nora looked at me as if I was a piece of mouldy bread. 'Don't they teach you anything these days? In 1918 it was only women over thirty who got the vote.'

'I'm sorry. I didn't know I was going to meet a ghost.'

Nora seemed to shrink, and I felt bad all over again.

'I really am sorry,' I said. 'What is it you want from me? Do you just want to – talk about things?' *What are you, Steph, a ghost therapist?* I'd seen occasional snippets of ghost-hunter shows while flicking through TV channels late at night, but I was pretty sure I'd never seen a ghost on the psychiatrist's couch. Those shows were more about vague noises, rattles and screams.

Nora gave me another contemptuous look, but then her expression softened. 'I want to right wrongs. I can't do it on my own, obviously. But *you* can open filing cabinets and get files and make notes. You could even make telephone calls. From a call box, I mean. The lines here shut down years ago.'

'Right.' I thought this over. 'But surely everyone involved is dead?'

'Not necessarily,' said Nora. 'I didn't say the injustices were all in *my* lifetime.'

'Uh-huh.' I folded my arms to keep them still as conflicting thoughts raced through my mind.

This is pointless. It won't help anyone.

It'll help Nora. Perhaps it will lay her soul to rest, and she won't have to see her home being demolished.

But it's such a waste of time.

And there's something better you could be doing?

28

At least you'd get to work on real cases. It could be good practice.

'All right,' I said. 'You're on.'

Nora gave me a sidelong glance. 'Really?'

'Yes, really. But I want you to promise, cross your heart and hope to die – oh heck, sorry – to promise that there won't be any weird stuff.'

Nora bit her lip. 'I promise *I* won't be weird. Is that good enough?'

'I suppose it'll have to do.' I held out a hand, side on. 'Shake on it.'

'I can't.' She demonstrated by moving her own hand through the table.

I could feel my face flushing. 'Er, good point. Um...' I moved my hand up and down slowly, then stopped.

Nora looked puzzled for a moment, then moved her own hand close to mine, so that the palms were almost touching. Together, we moved our hands slowly up and down. 'That's as good as a handshake, isn't it?' she said doubtfully.

I shrugged. 'I think so.'

'Marvellous!' She jumped up from her chair. 'I'll take you to the file room and we can get started.'

'Er, OK.' And I hurried along the corridor behind Nora, whose skirt would surely have swished if it had been real, wondering what on earth I'd got myself into.

CHAPTER 5

'You're joking,' I said as I gazed at a set of knackered-looking stairs that led to who knew what. 'I'm not going down there.'

'You've got to,' said Nora. 'That's where the file room is.'

'It's all right for you,' I said, hanging onto the warped banister and peering into the gloom. 'You don't weigh anything. If that collapses and I'm on it I could break my back.'

'You could take those big heavy boots off,' Nora suggested, eyeing them critically. 'That'd lose a few pounds.'

'Er, splinters? Cockroaches?'

'I'll have you know this was a well-kept station,' said Nora, gliding down the stairs. 'Come on, do. What a fuss you're making.'

I heaved a sigh and picked my way down, wincing at every groan and creak, and clutching at the banister as if it could possibly bear my weight in the event of a crisis. Somehow I reached the bottom without incident, and huffed out a relieved breath as I switched on my phone torch.

'There, that wasn't so bad, was it?' said Nora. 'We'll make a policewoman of you yet.'

'I am a policew— a police officer,' I said. 'Policewomen went out years ago.'

'Very modern, I'm sure,' Nora replied, with a sniff. 'This way. Oh, and watch out for that hole.' She waved her hand airily at two missing floorboards in the middle of the corridor.

I bit back a swearword. 'Good grief,' I said in disgust as I edged round the gap.

'I hope you brought your keys,' said Nora. 'I mean, it's all right for me, but you can't get through a locked door.' She waved a hand at a formidable blue door, on which was a tarnished brass plaque that said *FILE ROOM: PRIVATE.*

'Now she tells me,' I said, patting my pockets even though I knew the keys were in my bag upstairs. Or were they? I stuck my hand into my right trouser pocket, brought out the large, jingling ring, and stared at it. 'I could have sworn—'

'Please don't. Policewomen should set a good example.' Nora stood aside to let me pass her. The fifth key turned smoothly in the lock and the door opened with an ominous creak.

31

The file room was lined with dull grey metal filing cabinets. Several had dents in the bottom drawers. 'That's people kicking them shut,' said Nora, pointing. Dim cool light came from a barred skylight in the ceiling at the end of the room, and separated into rays which projected bars onto the large leather-covered table in the centre. Dust, disturbed by our entrance, danced briefly in the light before settling again.

'Where do we begin?' I asked, gazing around me.

'With a very strange case indeed,' said Nora. 'The case of the four fingers. The file's in one of those cabinets.' She indicated about half of the right-hand wall. 'I'll give you the gist while you look.'

'What am I looking for?' I asked. 'I assume it isn't filed under that.'

Nora giggled. 'That would make it easier, wouldn't it? It happened in the early sixties. Sixty-two? Sixty-three?'

'There's no point asking me,' I said, wrenching open the top drawer of the first cabinet and peering in.

Nora sat down, which was disconcerting as her chair was tucked neatly in and her chest protruded well into the table. 'It began on an evening in late October. I remember because turnip lanterns were in the front windows of the station.'

'Don't you mean pumpkins?'

Nora gave me a pitying glance. 'As I said, turnip

lanterns. It was quiet, as the pubs were still serving. Perhaps eight o'clock. Before nine, certainly.'

'That isn't very helpful.' The cases in the drawer, stored in buff-coloured cardboard folders, went from January to June 1962. I closed the drawer and opened the next one. At least they were filed in order.

'I'm setting the scene,' said Nora.

'Was it a dark and stormy night?'

Nora folded her arms. 'If you're going to make fun of me—'

'You're the one who's setting the scene,' I said. 'You keep talking, I'll look.'

'It was dark, obviously,' said Nora, 'but I don't remember any rain or wind. If anything, it was unusually nice for October.'

'Wonderful,' I muttered into the drawer.

'So I was on watch at the desk—'

I turned round again. 'You were dead, weren't you?'

Nora rolled her eyes. 'I was still on watch. A sergeant was there too, manning the desk. In fact, his name was Sergeant Manning.'

'That's lucky.'

'Yes, it is rather. A man came in, a local, holding a smallish white cardboard box like a cake box, and looking as if he'd stared death in the face.

"Are you all right, Bill?" asked the sergeant.

"I thought it might be an animal," said Bill. "An

abandoned kitten, or a puppy. Then I opened it and didn't know what to do, so I brought it here." He set the box on the desk and nudged it towards Sergeant Manning.

"So what is it?" asked the sergeant.

Bill folded his arms. "You look."

The sergeant lifted the lid and pushed it down with an oath. But in that moment I'd seen what was in the box.' Nora leaned forward, encroaching further into the table. '*Four severed fingers.*'

I grimaced. 'I won't find them in one of the cabinets, will I?'

'If you do, they'll probably be rotted to the bones by now,' said Nora. 'Like I will be.'

I stared at her, horrified. *What must it be like to know something like that?* I took a deep breath to get over that thought, and sneezed twice.

'I hope you're not coming down with a cold,' said Nora. 'If you are, you'd better rub your chest with goose fat, put brown paper on it and go to bed.'

'Why don't you carry on with the story,' I said. 'Did Bill say where he'd found them?'

'I was getting to that,' said Nora. 'He said the box was on top of a backyard wall, so anyone cutting through the alley would have seen it. "Imagine if a child had pulled it down," he said.'

'Was the box meant to be found?' I asked. 'Did people often take short cuts through alleys? I think this Bill sounds suspicious.'

Nora gave me a withering look. 'Course they did, and children played there too. Better than risking getting run over in the streets, isn't it?'

'I suppose.' I walked my fingers through the last of the files and closed the drawer, then opened the next. 'What else do you remember?'

'Well, this Bill asked if the sergeant would take fingerprints, and the sergeant laughed so hard he nearly fell off his chair. "If someone's lost four fingers we'll hear something soon enough," he said. "We'll enquire at the hospitals, and ask if any local doctors have had a visit from a man who needed his hand sewing up. Might have been a factory accident, or a nasty incident with a bacon slicer." Then he looked thoughtful. "Must remember to pick up sausages," he said.

"People can't go leaving boxes of fingers about!" cried Bill. He seemed pretty upset.'

'I'm not surprised,' I replied. 'I wouldn't react too well if I came across a box of fingers either.' I flicked through more files. September . . . October . . . October 15th . . . October 20th . . . October 23rd . . . 29th. I pulled the file out and inspected it. *MALICIOUS INJURY* was written on the front in neat block capitals.

'This is around the right date,' I said. I pulled out a chair and sat beside Nora at the table. 'Would you like me to pull that chair out for you a little?'

Nora shrugged. 'I'm fine. Let's look at the file.'

'Nora, you promised to try not to be weird...'

Nora heaved a sigh. 'Will pulling my chair out make you feel better?'

'Honestly? Yes, it would. I'm not used to working with people who can occupy the same place as the table they're working at.'

Nora stood up and waited while I moved her chair backwards. 'Thank you,' I said.

She sat down. 'Please can we get on?'

I opened the file.

Inside was a wodge of paper held loosely together by string tags. The first sheet was headed *SUMMARY*.

Date of incident: October 29, 1962.

Nature of incident: Four severed fingers brought to station.

Actions taken:

- *Statement taken from discoverer.*
- *Fingers photographed and prints recorded. No definite matches found in police records.*
- *Households close to location of discovery questioned. Possible suspect identified.*
- *Suspect arrested and charged.*
- *Case closed as suspect died while awaiting trial.*

'But who was the suspect?' cried Nora.

I paged through the file. 'According to this, someone called Tom Tinsley.'

Nora stared at me. 'It can't have been him,' she said, with a shake of her head as if she was trying to shake something loose. 'It just can't.'

CHAPTER 6

I studied Nora, who was wringing her hands on the table top. 'How do you mean, it can't be? How do you know that?'

'I don't know for sure,' said Nora, 'but it seems so unlikely. Tom Tinsley was a nice lad.'

'So you knew him?'

'Not exactly. I mean, how can you know someone when you can't speak to them and they don't know you're there? But he seemed nice.'

'Right.' I considered explaining that people who seemed nice weren't always nice, but decided I'd deserve whatever Nora said in reply. I settled for 'Let's look at the file together.'

We began with the statement, which was much as Nora had reported. Bill Cracknell was the proprietor of a local chandler's shop. He was taking a shortcut home when he saw the box glimmering in the moonlight. So far, so good. It was quiet, because he'd stayed on in his shop doing accounts after closing, and dark enough for children to be indoors.

'Nothing there, really,' I commented. I turned the page and almost cried out as I was faced with a full-colour photograph of the items Bill had handed in.

The image had the odd tones of an old photograph, unsurprisingly, with some colours washed out and others strangely intense. It didn't help. The fingers themselves were a sort of purplish grey. They had been photographed pointing towards the camera, which was something, but the nails were discoloured and the fingers bruised, as if they had been handled roughly. Then again, they had.

'Oh dear,' said Nora. 'Those don't look healthy.'

'I'm not surprised.' I peeked under the photograph and found another, this time taken from above. I had thought the fingers appeared short because of the angle of the first photo, but actually, they *were* short. Each had been cut off between the first and second joints. When I could bring myself to examine the cut finger ends, they were clean rather than jagged, as if they had been cut in one go. *Ugh.*

'Are there fingerprints?' asked Nora.

I turned the page gladly and found a page with four prints on it, each labelled. The smallest, presumably of the little finger, was slightly smudged.

Pasted on the bottom of the sheet was a typewritten piece of paper. *These prints have been checked against the police records and no distinct matches found.*

'Did they have fingerprinting in your day?' I asked.

'Of course they did,' said Nora. 'It had been around for about twenty years. That's like me asking you if you've heard of those fancy pocket calculators everyone's got nowadays.'

'Pocket calculators?' The penny dropped. 'Do you mean this?' I pulled my phone from my pocket and showed it to her.

'That's right. I don't know why you bother with them. They look fancy, but everyone I've seen with one moans that they don't work. You'd be better off with an adding machine.'

I considered explaining what I was actually holding and what it did, but there probably weren't enough hours in the day. Besides, we had a case to solve. 'Let's keep reading,' I said, and put the phone in my pocket.

Next came interviews with people from the immediate neighbourhood, but no one had seen or heard anything suspicious, either on the night in question or for a few days before. Enquiries at the local hospitals, doctors, factories and butchers had turned up nothing relevant.

'Did you, um, sit in on any of these interviews?' I asked.

Nora shook her head. 'I didn't want to get in the

way. What if a member of the public had seen me?'

I considered this. 'True. So why did they pick up this Tom character?'

'They needed someone to blame,' said Nora. 'Word got around and people were frightened. They had to arrest someone to calm everyone down. I heard them talking about it at the front desk when it was quiet.'

'I'll see what I can find in the local newspapers.' I said.

Nora snorted. 'I doubt there'll be anything. News round here spreads by word of mouth, mostly. Over the back wall, in queues at the shops, hanging out your washing. Or it did.'

I decided against explaining the World Wide Web and rolling news. 'I'll try, anyway: you never know. I'll have to do that somewhere else, though. Somewhere I can get hold of the newspapers.'

'Oh, like the public library? Do they still have those?'

I smiled. 'Just about.'

'I used to love the library,' said Nora. 'I'd go to Kensington Library once a week, borrow as many books as I could carry, and read in bed when I'd finished work. Mum used to complain something shocking about the waste of candles, and my sisters whined that they couldn't sleep.'

I goggled at her. 'You shared a bedroom?'

Nora stared back at me. 'Of course I did. There were five of us girls and one bedroom. You can't make that any different, even with your fancy calculator.' She grinned. 'Luckily two of my sisters worked nights, so there were only ever three of us in there at one time.'

I shuddered. Sharing a bunk bed with my sister on holiday had been hell on earth when we were kids. I took out my notebook and wrote *29 October 1962* and *Check local newspapers*. Then I turned to the next page of the file. 'Oh.'

The next sheet of paper looked as if it had been used to wrap food. It was shiny and near-transparent in places, presumably from butter or grease, and even after all these years the folds were clearly visible. But the words were the important thing.

DEER POLIS,

IF YOUR LOOKING FOR WHO CUT OFF THEM FINGERS, CHECK THE POKETS OF YOUR FREIND YOUNG TOM.

YOU'LL FIND A SHARP NIFE BUT NOT A CLEER CONSHUNS.

A WELL WISHER

Nora gasped. 'Was that it? Was that why they pulled him in?'

'I suppose so.' I felt dazed. Perhaps the stale air

and the dust were getting to me.

The note had been scrawled in capital letters, using a pencil. On the back was another typewritten label. *This note was pushed under the door of the police station sometime during the night of 31st October. No fingerprints found.*

'That's suspicious for a start.' Nora was literally bristling. I suspected that if I'd been able to touch her I'd have got an electric shock.

'Maybe whoever wrote it was worried about Tom coming after them,' I said. 'I mean, if they genuinely thought he'd done it—'

'Rubbish!' cried Nora. 'That lad wouldn't have hurt a fly.'

'You still haven't explained how you know that.'

Nora's bottom lip trembled slightly. 'I didn't know I was on trial too.'

'Oh, Nora, don't be silly.' She bristled at that. 'I'm sorry, but I'm just trying to find out the truth, and it's really hard when everyone's probably dead. And your colleague definitely is.'

Nora slumped in her chair. 'I s'pose.' Then her frame stiffened. 'What time is it?'

I looked at the clock on the wall, but it had stopped. I checked my watch. 'Nearly half past nine. I didn't realise we'd been here that long—'

Nora stood up. 'We must go upstairs.'

I stared at her. 'Why?'

'There isn't time to ask questions!' Nora hurried to the door and put her head through it, then drew back and looked at me. 'I can't hear him yet. We still have time. Quickly!'

'Nora, I don't mind taking the file upstairs. I just want to know why.'

'Oh, go boil your head.' And Nora vanished through the door.

Shaking my own head, I closed the file and took my time making sure that everything was as it had been when we arrived. Only then did I tuck the file under my arm and leave, locking the door behind me.

I took my time on the stairs, too, using my phone light and testing each step before I put my weight on it. I was looking forward to being on solid ground again. *At least I won't have to go back for a while*, I thought. *Maybe never. In a fortnight it'll be gone, anyway.*

What would they do with the records? Would they scan them, or move them to an offsite storage facility? Maybe they'd decide the records were no further use and shred them. I imagined the files being fed into a huge industrial shredder, and a cold shudder went through me.

I saw Nora peeking round the corner. She put a finger to her lips, then drew back so that I couldn't see her. That suited me fine. I didn't want to talk to Nora anyway. *I can't work with someone who runs off when*

44

I ask questions she doesn't fancy answering.

I went to the main room and put the kettle on. Tea was definitely in order. Nora hovered in the doorway, but I didn't speak to her until I had made tea, sat down, and helped myself to a biscuit. 'What's going on?'

Nora folded her arms. 'Nothing.'

'People don't run away from nothing. And if you don't tell me, I won't help you.' I patted the file on the table next to me. 'I can go to the superintendent's office with this and read it in peace on my own. Or even better, I could read my book. That would be more use to me than digging up some cold case where they probably got the right person anyway.'

'No!' cried Nora. 'You have to help me.'

'I don't.' Nora looked absolutely stricken. 'All right. Tell me why you ran out of the file room and I'll think about it.'

'You didn't see him?'

'See who?'

'The superintendent. He always goes to the file room at nine thirty in the morning. But you can't have seen him, or you'd have got out of his way on the stairs.'

I remembered how I'd shuddered, and did it again. 'Did he walk through me?'

Nora looked uncomfortable. 'I'm afraid he did.'

'You could have warned me! Why didn't you say

something?'

'He'd have heard me,' she muttered.

'Why would that matter? You're one of his staff.'

'We didn't get on.' The words burst out of Nora. 'I stay away from him. I can't—' She vanished.

I drank some tea, but it might as well have been hot water for all the good it did me. 'Honestly!' I banged the mug down and it slopped tea onto the table. *You have every right to be angry*, I told myself. But it wasn't just anger. And beneath it, I was deeply uneasy.

CHAPTER 7

For some time after Nora had gone – I didn't want to say the word vanished – I drank my tea and fumed. What a waste of time it was, being stuck here. What sort of colleague would keep information from me and refuse to tell me what, if anything, she knew about an investigation?

You could just read the file.

My hand moved, then stopped in mid-air. Would that bring Nora back? What would happen then? *If she comes back, I'll go to the superintendent's office. She can't follow me there, because of the horses.* That made me feel guilty. *It's not my fault,* I argued to myself. *I'm not setting them on her. And it might be an excuse, anyway.* I remembered the horrible chill I'd felt on the basement stairs. *Whatever.* I pulled the file towards me and opened it.

The next few pages gave more detail about Tom Tinsley. He was eighteen, and worked as a butcher's assistant in a shop down the road. He lived at home with his parents above their draper's shop.

The police must have taken the anonymous letter seriously, for Sergeant Manning had taken more statements. Two people had mentioned seeing Tom Tinsley waving a large knife in a dark alley, muttering to himself and laughing. 'I don't know whether that's anything to do with this fingers business, but it's odd,' one witness had said. 'Prancing around like that. And him a butcher's boy. Used to handling a knife.' Understandably, neither had confronted him.

Another short report followed, in which Tom Tinsley was pulled in for questioning. When asked about what witnesses had seen, he did not confirm or deny it, or provide an alibi for 29th October or the nights preceding it. His repeated reply was 'A fellow's got a right to his own free time, hasn't he?'

I sighed in exasperation. *Why wouldn't he help himself? Why didn't he say what he was doing?*

The next document was a transcription of an interview with Tinsley's parents. They confirmed that Tom had returned late on the evening of the 29th. When asked whether this was usual, his mother had said 'Not really. Though he has come in late these past few days.' The police officer interviewing them had added, in brackets, *Mother seemed worried.*

I bet she did, I thought. On the face of it, Tom Tinsley appeared guilty as could be. But Nora's certainty made me pause. Why was she so sure that he was the wrong man?

The next document dealt with Tom Tinsley's arrest. Sergeant Manning and Constable Jeffreys had arrested him at the butcher's shop and marched him to the station, where he was confronted with the fingers.

When the suspect was shown the box of severed fingers he looked horrified, the report said. *Tinsley said 'That weren't me, I wouldn't do that.' However, after a while his expression changed from horror to something else. On discussion afterwards, the constable and I thought it might be fascination.*

Given his behaviour and witness testimony, Inspector Tasker judged it prudent not to offer bail, but to place Tinsley in a cell pending trial. The suspect was unhappy about this and attempted to leave the police station. It took three of us to hold Tinsley down, for he was tall and strong.

A report from the police surgeon followed:

REGARDING THOMAS TINSLEY. I examined this man to the best of my ability on the morning of 2nd November. I say to the best of my ability, because he refused to let me touch him. He appeared in good health and of normal weight. However, the knuckles of his right hand were bruised and swollen. He admitted he had been punching the wall of his cell. He was seething with rage and would not be reasoned with. He refused to answer my questions, though I

*said they might help him. 'I've had enough of help,'
he said. 'That's what's put me here.' When asked to
explain this comment, he shook his head, sat in the
corner of the cell and put his head in his hands.*

*I cannot comment on his usual mental state but
such a display of wilful anger and senseless violence,
combined with his size and strength, are an extremely
dangerous combination. I recommend that Tinsley
remains in solitary confinement until an expert
opinion is obtained. This should take place in a
secure environment.*

Below the surgeon's signature was a handwritten
note. *Tinsley taken to HMP Walton 5th Nov. Awaiting
trial date.*

There was only one more page in the file. It was
typewritten.

*10th November: informed by the prison governor
that Thomas Tinsley was found dead in his cell this
morning. He refused to eat or drink despite the best
efforts of the wardens, and dashed himself against the
walls of his cell until he was restrained. Sergeant
Manning will inform his family.*

*As no other suspects have been identified, this case
is now closed.*

I closed the file feeling cheated, as if I had binge-
watched a TV show and the last episode had been
deleted before I got to it. 'That can't be it,' I muttered.

50

'That can't be all there is.' I half-wished Nora would come back.

I sat for a long time, trying to piece together the parts of the jigsaw, till my stomach roused me with an ominous rumble.

I looked at my watch. Twelve o'clock. Close enough.

'I'm going out to get some lunch,' I said, for the benefit of anyone who might be listening. There was no response, not even a breeze. I picked up my bag and phone and left, putting a *Back Soon* notice on the front door.

I bought a chicken salad baguette and a Diet Coke from the shop round the corner, then stood on the pavement, unsure of what to do. I just knew that I didn't want to go straight back to the Bridewell. I wanted to be anywhere else, rather than alone with my thoughts. Could anywhere – or anyone – help me? And almost of their own accord, my feet carried me to Erskine Street police station.

'She's back!' said Huw as I came into the main office. 'Bored of the Bridewell already, Steph?'

'It isn't the liveliest place I've ever worked in,' I said. 'I had a look around, though. There's interesting stuff downstairs in the file room.'

'Is there?' He laughed. 'I didn't know there was a file room.'

Sam Davies glanced up from her computer. 'You

shouldn't poke about in that old dump. I told you it wasn't safe.'

'It was fine,' I said, crossing my fingers behind my back. 'Just a couple of missing floorboards.'

Huw's grin widened. 'What were you hoping to find, Steph? Buried treasure? Or were you looking for a case?'

I nodded.

'That's very diligent of you, I must say. What did you find?'

'Well, there was a case from the sixties where someone found four fingers in a box, but it never went to trial.'

'How come?' said Tasha Saunders, turning on her chair.

'The only suspect, um… He died.'

'So they didn't manage to catch anyone . . . *red-handed?*' Huw and Sam exchanged glances and sniggered.

'Very funny,' I said. 'I might check out some old newspapers, in case that gives me any ideas. A new angle on things.'

'That's a good idea,' said Tasha.

'It is, actually,' said Huw. 'But there's something that could be even more helpful.'

'Really?' I tried to hide my surprise that he was taking me seriously.

'Yeah.' He stood up. 'I'll show you. Sam, want to

come?'

Sam shrugged, a puzzled expression on her face. 'If you like.'

Huw led us down the corridor. 'You probably shouldn't mention this to the inspector. It's for sergeants and above, but seeing as you're on a case… Is this your first case?'

'The first one I'm leading on, yes,' I said, slightly breathless from my efforts to keep up.

'Excellent. Not far now.' He rounded a corner and stopped in front of a door. 'Here we are.' He waved at the door. 'After you.'

I opened the door and found myself looking into a broom cupboard. 'What the—'

'Don't be so quick to judge,' said Huw. 'You'll find it on the back shelves, second from top.'

I craned my neck. 'I'll find what?' *What could it be? Discs with old files on them? Microfilm?*

'The time machine!' Huw let out a bark of laughter.

Sam leaned against him, giggling. 'Your face, Steph!'

I stepped back and closed the door, then returned to my desk and gathered my things. They followed, hovering nearby.

'It was only a joke.'

'Come on, Steph, you've got to admit that was funny.'

I glared at them, which made them dissolve into giggles. 'You may find it funny, but a man died during that case – *because* of that case – and I'm not sure he was guilty. I'll do my best to find out what I can, and I don't care what you think about it.' I walked out of the office, untouched chicken baguette in hand, and headed for the Bridewell.

CHAPTER 8

I hadn't walked more than a few metres when someone called 'Steph!'

It didn't sound like Huw, or Sam. I turned and saw Tasha hurrying towards me. 'I just heard about what Huw did. He won't apologise, but I want to say sorry on his behalf.'

'It wasn't your fault.' I shrugged. 'I should have known better than to say anything. I suppose you think I'm wasting my time, too.'

'No— Well, not really. I mean, what else is there to do? It isn't as if anyone ever brings anything interesting to the Bridewell. Maybe you will find something out, although I'm not sure how.'

'Me neither.' We were standing in the middle of the pavement and people gave us curious glances as they skirted round us. 'And now I'll be made fun of at Erskine Street if I do any research.'

'I'll defend you.' Tasha drew herself up. 'They

can't expect someone like you to sit around all day.'

I smiled. 'Someone like me?'

Tasha looked at her feet, then at me. 'Yeah, you know. Busy.'

'Um, thanks. Anyway, I'd better get back there. Before the queue gets too long.'

'I can walk down with you—'

'No, it's fine. You've got stuff to do.' The speed of my response surprised me. I imagined Tasha coming into the Bridewell with me and encountering Nora.

'Are you all right?' Tasha took a step closer. 'Are you sure you don't want me to walk with you?'

'I'm fine. Really.' I shifted from foot to foot. 'I'm probably hungry. Not to mention bored.' I grinned. 'I should have taken advantage of the station wi-fi, seeing as I can't even get a signal at the Bridewell.'

'You can.'

I raised my eyebrows. 'Can you?'

Tasha looked shifty. It suited her. 'You know the yard? If you stand under the iron steps you can get two bars.'

'That's good to know. I should go, though. Thanks, Tasha.'

'No problem,' said Tasha, and I made off, armed with my new knowledge and a renewed sense of purpose.

I made sure the front door of the Bridewell was firmly closed before speaking. 'Nora?' I called. There was no reply.

I walked into the main room and nearly swore as I clapped eyes on Nora. She was sitting in what I thought of as my chair, with her elbows on the table and her chin on her hands.

'Most people say hello,' I said, once I'd recovered.

'I didn't know if you were coming back,' said Nora. 'I thought you might not bother. Seeing as this place will be knocked down anyway.'

'Let me fill the kettle, and we'll talk.' When I picked it up there was enough water for at least one cup of tea, but I wanted time to think. *What do I say to her?* 'I'll be back in two minutes.'

I climbed the stairs slowly. *How does she know?* Then I realised she could hardly *not* know. The developers would have visited the station, no doubt commenting as they went round, and I suspected the police officers on duty lately would have spoken their minds. After all, who would hear?

I turned the tap on savagely and was rewarded with a stream of water so forceful that it rebounded from the kettle and splashed my jumper. 'Brilliant,' I said, turning the tap down. 'Just brilliant.' I dabbed at myself with a paper towel and went downstairs.

Nora looked marginally less glum than she had when I first came in. I plugged in the kettle, switched it on and sat down. 'What have you heard?' I asked.

'What do you know?' Nora countered.

'Only hearsay. You've probably heard it too. Sam told me they're selling the Bridewell soon and it'll be made into luxury flats.'

'Huh,' said Nora.

'Were you there when Sam showed me round?' I remembered the draught in the cell.

'No,' said Nora. 'I was in the file room.'

'You weren't in the cells?'

Nora shook her head. 'Why would I go there? I'm not a criminal.'

'Oh, OK. It's just that I felt a cold wind when we went inside one, and Sam didn't. She asked if I was all right.'

'Is Sam the one with short grey hair?'

'That's her.'

Nora wrinkled her nose. 'I'm not surprised *she* didn't notice anything. I've sat on her lap before now, trying to get a response out of her. She might as well be dead, that one.'

'That's a bit harsh.' The kettle boiled and I poured hot water into the mug, then remembered I hadn't put a teabag in. 'So if it wasn't you in the cell, who was it?' I scrabbled in the packet and dunked the teabag with my spoon.

'It won't have been a – what do you say? A police officer,' said Nora. 'I reckon it was who I said. A criminal. Well, not a real criminal. The people who we locked up for the night were mostly drunk, disorderly, or begging. And if they were women and not locked up for one of those three things, you can probably guess what they were doing.'

'Do you have any idea who it could be?' I asked, partly to change the subject.

Nora shook her head. 'Anyone on the wrong side of the law who haunts this place stays away from the likes of me. Unpleasant memories, I suppose.'

I flicked my teabag into the bin and added milk to my mug. 'Nora, will you be honest with me?'

Nora looked even shiftier than Tasha had. 'It depends. What about?'

'Why are you so sure that Tom Tinsley was innocent?'

Her face cleared. 'Whenever he came into the station he seemed like a nice person. A gentle person.'

'Why did he come into the station?' In my head, I ran over the reasons Nora had mentioned.

Nora frowned at me. 'It wasn't that. Sometimes he was a bit tipsy on a Friday night after he'd been paid, but Sergeant Manning just used to confiscate his pay packet, send him packing, and drop what was left of his wages in to his mother the next day. But he wasn't mean when he was drunk, nor angry. Silly, yes. Likely to fall off his chair when he was trying to focus on the sergeant, but nothing worse. He used to bring in young birds that had fallen out of their nests, or little injured animals, and ask if he could put them by the radiator and have food scraps and water for them. He said his family would laugh at him if he took them home. So for a lad like that to do a thing like that, it's not right.'

'I see what you mean,' I said. 'Unless – I'm no expert, you understand – unless he had a split personality, or some kind of mental breakdown?'

'That'd be handy, wouldn't it?' said Nora, her tone bitter. 'That would explain everything.'

'It's just a theory.' I reflected on what I'd read earlier. 'The police surgeon seemed to think he was fine when he checked him out. Apart from being very angry.'

'I'd be angry if I was arrested for something I hadn't done,' said Nora.

'True. But I'd be sensible and help the police, to have more chance of being released.'

'*You* would. You know the system. You've got an education – a proper one, not out on your ear at twelve or thirteen like me and my sisters. The poor lad probably thought the world was against him. No one ever visited him. His parents were only a few doors away, and they never came once.'

'All right, all right!' I raised my hands. 'You can't blame me for reading the case file.'

'You can't blame me for knowing what I saw,' Nora replied. She watched me for a few moments.

'Are you going to drink that tea?'

I took a sip, then set the mug down. 'I miss tea,' said Nora, whose gaze was fixed on the mug the whole time. 'So does this mean you're back on the case?'

'I suppose it does.' I took another sip and studied Nora over the rim of the mug. 'I found some information that could help us.' I considered trying to explain online newspaper archives, and decided it was beyond me. 'Getting hold of newspapers might be easier than I thought.'

'That's good,' said Nora, but I could tell her mind was elsewhere. 'I wonder who was in that cell. Can you recall which one you visited?'

I thought for a moment. 'One of the middle ones. I'm not sure which.' Nora was gazing at me. 'What do you have in mind?'

'Whoever's in there may know something about this case,' said Nora. 'Will you go and see if you can speak to them?'

'On one condition,' I replied.

Nora's eyes opened even wider. 'What's that?'

I tapped the chicken baguette. 'That I can eat my lunch first.'

CHAPTER 9

With my grumbling stomach finally satisfied, I led the way towards the cells. Then I stopped in the middle of the corridor. 'Which way is it? I know it's one of the doors, but which?'

Nora pointed at a door. 'That one.'

'Oh, OK.' I opened it and walked down the short corridor of cells. 'Maybe that one?' I said, pointing to the middle door. But Nora hadn't followed me in. She was standing in the doorway. I'd say hovering, but her feet were on the floor. 'Aren't you coming?'

Nora took a tentative step forward. 'I didn't have much to do with the cells. I was mostly out on the beat.'

'Oh.' I thought this over. Was it something to do with the superintendent she ran away from? Maybe it was sexism from her male colleagues, who assumed Nora wouldn't be able to cope with actual offenders, or perhaps misplaced delicacy made them shrink from asking her to do such work. 'I could do with a hand, so if you don't mind—'

Nora edged along the corridor, much as I had done on the way to the file room. 'Well, then,' she said, gazing at the door.

'Here goes nothing,' I said, and opened it.

The cell looked identical to the one I had visited – had it been only yesterday? I paced around it, waiting for the chilly breeze to strike, but I felt nothing. 'Can you see or feel anyone, Nora?'

Nora shook her head from the doorway. 'Not a thing.'

'Are you coming in?'

She shook her head again, more forcibly this time.

'OK. Shall we try the next cell?'

'If you want,' said Nora, taking a step back to let me pass. 'Make sure you close that door properly.'

'Yes ma'am.' I sighed as I drew the bolt and turned the key in the lock. I didn't mind taking orders from my seniors, but ghosts were a different matter. 'What rank did you hold in the service, if you don't mind me asking?'

Nora eyed my uniform. 'You're a constable, aren't you?'

'That's right.' I walked to the next cell. 'Were you a WPC?'

Nora gave a curt nod.

'So we're equals.'

'My service is considerably longer than yours,' said Nora. 'So I'm senior.'

I snorted. 'I'm not sure you can count the years you've been dead as actual service, Nora. Not really.' I unlocked the cell and pushed the door open.

Cold air hit me in the face and I jumped, then turned my face away. *Imagine if you breathed something in.* 'This is the one. I'm sure of it.'

I moved to the middle of the cell, making sure that my hands were visible and open. 'Is anyone there?' I felt like a medium in a comedy sketch. 'Please show yourself. I promise not to hurt you.'

I've heard that before. The response echoed round me in a chilly whisper.

'I – we – won't hurt you. Will we, Nora?'

You have to catch me first. The whisper came from the direction of the high window. *How has it got up there?*

'I don't want to catch you. I just want to speak to you.'

They all say that.

I saw a sort of mist around the window ledge, which gradually resolved itself into a man-sized shape, and sharpened into a small, wizened figure dressed in clothes little better than rags.

'Er, hello.' I tried a tentative wave. 'Could you tell me your name, please?'

The figure waved a hand. 'If you wish to know,

64

you can consult the records.' He looked past me to Nora. 'What does she want?'

'We're trying to investigate an old case,' I said. 'As you'll appreciate, it's quite difficult—'

'Because you've got no body to talk to!' The ghost wheezed with laughter, sagging sideways till I thought he would fall off the windowsill.

I managed to smile. 'Precisely. I felt your presence the other day, and wondered whether you'd witnessed anything.'

The ghost cocked his head at me. 'Maybe. Is there a reward?'

'Erm, what would you like?'

'That's a good question.' The ghost scratched his head, thinking. 'I'd like to get out of here, but I can't. I can pass through the door, but the door at the end is barred.' He focused on Nora. 'I'm surprised to see you.'

'I'm with her,' said Nora, glaring at him.

I looked from one to the other. 'So you two know each other?'

'In a manner of speaking,' said Nora, with a sneer. 'Alf Doolittle here was what you might call one of our regulars. And no, that wasn't his real name, but that's what everyone called him. What was it? Dooley? Dolan?'

'Duchamp,' said the old man. 'Jack Duchamp. My dad was French, not that I knew him.'

I sensed the conversation veering off-topic. 'Did you ever see a young man called Tom Tinsley in your cell?'

Jack raised his eyes to the ceiling. 'I've seen more people in this cell than I've had hot dinners. Considerably more. That's why I kept ending up here: drinking on an empty stomach. If I just had sixpence for a nice hot meal o' nights, I could drink like a lord.'

'If you didn't spend your money on drink, you could get a hot meal every night,' Nora shot back.

I looked up at the ghost, who was swinging his legs. 'Jack, if you can tell me anything about Tom Tinsley, I'll do my best to get you out of this corridor.'

Jack looked down his snub nose at me. 'Is that a promise?'

'I promise I'll try. I can't promise it'll work.'

'Go on then.' Without warning, Jack launched himself from the window ledge and dropped onto the floor. I feared for his bones until I realised he didn't really have any. 'Let's see the colour of your money.'

'Can I have a word outside?' asked Nora.

'Here we go,' said Jack. 'I suppose you want to keep me locked up, Nora.' He winked at me. 'She's no fun.'

Nora ignored him and beckoned to me. I followed her into the main corridor. 'What is it?'

'Don't let him out,' said Nora. 'If you do, he'll leave the station and you'll never see him again. I know Jack. I've known him since he was a young man, teasing me whenever they brought him in. He'd promise you the earth if he thought there was a penny in it for him.'

'I need to offer him something or he won't talk to us. How about if I let him into this bit of the corridor?'

Nora snorted. 'You can try, but don't say I didn't warn you. He might look like a bundle of rags, but he can move pretty fast when he wants.'

I returned to the cell corridor, where I found Jack waiting. 'OK, I'll give it a go.' Feeling supremely silly, I raised a hand. 'Jack Duchamp, as the senior police officer—'

Nora coughed, eyebrows raised.

'All *right*, Nora – the senior *living* police officer of the Bridewell – I grant you a pass to enter the main corridor of this building and move not more than three feet in any direction.'

Jack put his hands in his pockets and ambled towards the door. He slowed as he reached it. 'This is where I normally come unstuck.' He stopped and raised his left foot, then brought it slowly forward. 'Oooh.' He put his foot down, bent his knees and jumped through the doorway.

I heard him laugh. Nora shouted, 'He's going to run!'

'Oof,' Jack gasped, and Nora giggled.

I entered the main corridor to find Jack rubbing his forehead. 'It worked, then,' I said.

Jack gave me a rueful look. 'I'll say it did.' He gazed around him at the debris stacked against the walls. 'Can't say I like what you've done with the place, but it's nice to see it again after all these years.'

'Now then, Jack,' said Nora. 'Cough up.'

'All right.' Jack straightened up, his hands by his sides, suddenly like an old soldier. 'Tom Tinsley were never in my cell.'

Nora hissed.

'Hold up. He were definitely in the cell next door, for I heard the sawbones talking to him. "Speak to me, Tinsley," he said, and "Why did you do it?", and "Where's the rest of him?"'

'What did Tom say?' I breathed.

'He said "I never done nothing," and I thought to myself, oh dear oh dear, that's the wrong thing to say. Coppers always pick up on them double negatives. They're tricksy.'

'But you knew him?' I asked.

'By sight, yes. I saw him out and about – sometimes he stood me a drink, if I asked nicely – and he seemed a decent enough lad. Couldn't handle his drink, though. Not like me.' He gave me a sharp look. 'What's he done? Or not done?'

'He was supposed to have cut off someone's fingers,' said Nora. 'But we don't think it was him.'

'Fingers?' Jack raised his left hand and stared at it, or possibly through it. 'Someone wanted one of mine once. Said they'd pay me for it. A whole pound, if you can believe it. Didn't like the sound of it much, so I turned 'em down.'

Nora leaned forward. 'Who? Tell us!'

Jack took a step back. 'That I can't do.'

Nora tried to grab him by the shoulders but her grip went straight through. 'Why not? Did they threaten you?'

'I'll thank you to take your hands off me,' said Jack, with an attempt at dignity. 'I can't tell you because I don't know. It was dark, for one thing, and my last drink had disagreed with me, so I was having a little rest in the gutter. All I can tell you is that they had scarves wrapped round their faces, and hats pulled low, and one was big and one small. That's how I know I wasn't seeing double – they was different sizes. The big one spoke first. "Fancy helping us out?" he said, in a husky sort of voice. When I turned him down he tried to get hold of me, but I wriggled so much that he dropped me. "Leave it," muttered the little 'un. "You'll make a row and bring someone down on us. I've got a better idea." And off they stomped. I went back to sleep, and by the time I woke I wasn't sure if it was a dream or not.'

'Can you remember when it happened?' I asked. I glanced at Nora, who was staring at him with her mouth open.

'Not the date, nor the day: don't have much use for those. I'd say it was a few days before I heard the doc trying to get answers out of Tom Tinsley.' He gazed at me pathetically. 'Will you let me go? I've told you all I know.'

'Are you sure?' asked Nora. 'Are you absolutely sure?'

'Look at this face,' said Jack, attempting to point to it and missing. 'Would I lie to you?'

Nora shrugged. 'I don't think he knows any more than that. You might as well.'

I raised my hand again, but when I looked at Jack it was hard to focus on him.

'Hello,' said Jack, 'what's all this? Oh, that feels nice.' I could barely see him now.

I turned to Nora. 'What's happening?'

'I think he's done what he needed to,' she said, not taking her eyes off him. 'He's going to his rest.'

We both watched Jack fade, until with a last whispered 'Blimey!' he disappeared completely.

CHAPTER 10

I felt a rush of air next to me and whipped round. Was it Jack, returning?

No, it was Nora, jumping up and down with a huge grin on her face. 'We've got suspects! We've got suspects!'

'I suppose we have.' She looked like a small child who had been given a treat. 'Didn't that bother you?'

Nora stopped jumping. 'What?'

'Jack disappearing.'

Nora shrugged. 'He seemed happy enough. Wouldn't you want a break after hanging around this place for however many years it's been? He spent so much time in the cells that he probably barely noticed when he died.'

'That's awful,' I said. 'But what happens now?'

Nora's grin was back. 'We investigate!'

'Yes, but—'

'Come on! Let's go to the detective office!'

Nora fidgeted as I locked doors and checked them. 'I don't know why you bother, Steph. It's not as if anyone's coming in and out, is it?'

'It's the right thing to do,' I said as I followed her down the corridor. 'Hang on, let me get a cuppa first.'

'I'll wait here,' said Nora, sitting on the second step of the staircase. 'I can't bear to watch you messing around. There's no time to lose!'

'Nora, this case has been dormant for what, sixty years? Two minutes either way won't make a difference.'

Nora folded her arms and set her jaw. I rolled my eyes and went back to the main room.

As I listened to the kettle rumbling into life I reviewed what we'd learnt. Two men – at least I presumed they were men – one big, one small, who'd wanted to cut off one of Jack's fingers. It wasn't much to go on.

Although if they'd only wanted one of Jack's fingers... The kettle pinged and I poured the water so hastily that I overfilled the mug. 'Aargh!' I mopped up, made tea, grabbed the case file and my notebook, and hastened out.

Nora was already in the office, studying the blank noticeboard. 'Don't tell me there are ghost notices on there,' I said.

She turned round. 'Don't be silly. We could pin bits of paper on it. About the case.'

'Instead of a whiteboard, you mean?'

'What's a whiteboard?'

'Never mind. I've thought of something. If those men just wanted one of Jack's fingers, that suggests the four fingers aren't from the same person.' I plumped down in the armchair and opened the file, riffling through it for the photographs. 'Let's look again.'

Nora peered at the photo. 'They seem pretty similar to me.'

I inspected the photo too. 'That could be the colour processing.' I sighed. 'I thought we were getting somewhere.'

'We might be,' said Nora. 'I tell you what, though.'

I looked up from the file. 'What?'

'We need a proper table, and another chair. We can't be expected to work in conditions like this.'

I visualised the cramped office where I spent most of my time. It had facilities Nora could only have dreamed of. 'OK, where do I find a table and chairs?'

'The next office has more furniture,' said Nora. 'You could try there.'

I picked up the file. 'Or we could move in there.'

'I like this one better,' said Nora. 'It's got the best view.'

I pushed aside the stained net curtain and gazed out at a leaden sky and a section of Liverpool skyline. Some buildings were still works in progress. Every so often a crane moved, like the second hand of a clock. 'Oh yes, I see what you mean. Enviable.' I let the curtain fall. 'I'll look, but I'm promising nothing.'

I got up and Nora immediately took my place. 'Good hunting,' she said, crossing her ankles.

I shook my head as I walked down the corridor. *Talk about cheek. No wonder Nora and the superintendent didn't see eye to eye, if this is what she was like when she was alive.* I tried the next door down, which was unlocked.

This room was in a worse state, with peeling paint and broken tiles on the fireplace, but it held a table and two upright chairs. I sighed, stacked the chairs, and took them to the door. *She'd better say thank you.*

Nora jumped up and clapped her hands in delight when I appeared in the doorway. 'Wonderful!' she cried, and I felt mean for my bad temper. 'Is there a table?'

'Yes, I'm going to get it.' I turned, then thought of something. 'Hang on a minute. Why don't you know if there's a table next door? How many years have you been here?'

Nora shrugged. 'Not my office, not my business.'

I studied her, but her expression didn't change. 'Whatever. I'll be back in a minute.' *I'm glad I wasn't a police officer a hundred years ago. Everyone has their own territory, almost.*

I dragged the table along the corridor and into our

office. 'I think it would look good there,' said Nora, pointing to the wall beneath the noticeboard.

'Oh, do you?' I said, though I agreed. I pushed it against the wall and placed the two chairs.

'Now we can really work!' said Nora, sitting down and rubbing her hands.

I smiled. 'I suppose we can.' I transferred everything onto the table, including my tea and the beer mat, then opened my notebook. *Four fingers may not be from the same person*, I wrote at the top of a fresh page. Then underneath: *But who?*

'Not Jack, obviously,' said Nora.

'No.' I wrote *Jack* and put a line through it. 'How can we find out? If they were preying on drunks and vagrants, would those people go anywhere for treatment afterwards?'

'They could go to the ozzy,' said Nora.

'The what?'

Nora rolled her eyes. 'Hospital. That's what I'd do. I'd make up something about catching my hand in machinery.'

'And the police wouldn't pick it up because they were looking for four fingers, not one.'

'Or they could put iodine and a bandage on it and carry on,' said Nora. 'That way, there wouldn't be any awkward questions.'

I winced. 'I hope they didn't.' I thought. 'Maybe we should search for hospital admissions with gangrene to the hand over the next few weeks. That's if the records still exist.'

'Hmmm,' said Nora. 'If you don't mind me saying, you're going down a rabbit hole.'

'So you don't think it's important to track down where – who – the fingers came from?'

'I'm not saying that isn't important, but it isn't as if we're giving them back, is it? Why did these two men want them? That's the question.'

I shrugged. 'Presumably, to put in a box.'

'To frame someone? Tom Tinsley?'

'It's likely: whoever found the box was bound to take it to the police. But why bother? And did they write the anonymous letter, or was it someone else?'

'I don't know,' said Nora. 'Let's look at it.' I found the letter in the file and Nora's lips moved as she read it. 'Whoever wrote this wasn't a very good speller.'

'Or they were pretending not to be.' I rubbed the stained paper between my fingers. 'I wonder where this came from.'

'Pinched it, probably,' said Nora. 'Whoever wrote and delivered this knew what they were doing. They wore gloves. No fingerprints.' She frowned. 'That's odd.'

'What is?'

Nora inspected the paper. 'This is shop wrapping paper, so it was handed to them by someone. You'd expect prints from whoever handled it first, and there aren't any. So that person wore gloves too.'

'True.' I ran my finger down the edge of the paper. 'What sorts of things were wrapped in paper like this?'

'It's just rough paper. You'd expect newspaper for fish and chips, or waxed paper for other food. There's no dirt on it. So maybe household goods?'

'Can you remember what shops were nearby, Nora?'

She shook her head. 'Not after my time. We need a street directory.' She looked around the room. 'Another office might have one. Or you could try the file room.'

'I'll go and see.' I checked the other two offices, which were bare of books. *The file room it is*, I thought. *But where?*

I returned to our office. 'Nora, where would I find —'

'*Sshhhh.*' Nora was rigid, her gaze fixed on the door. She was also slightly more transparent than usual.

'What's up?'

'Oh heck, it's him,' Nora breathed, and dived behind the armchair.

A foot came through the door, followed by an upright, elderly man in an old-fashioned suit, with a bristling moustache and slicked-back grey hair. He came to a stop, gazed around him, then glared at me.

'Where is she?' he barked.

'Who?' I asked. 'And who might you be?'

'You know very well who I mean,' the man snapped. 'And you ought to know that I am Superintendent Hicks, and I am in charge.' He looked me up and down. 'Who gave you permission to wear those?'

He was glaring at my trousers. 'They're regulation uniform, Superintendent.' I wasn't calling him sir, not for anything. And I had no idea why I could see him now when I hadn't been able to that morning.

'Not on my watch they aren't,' said the superintendent. 'Stop distracting me. Where is she? Is she hiding in here? And don't give me any flannel, I heard you talking.' He marched around the room, peering under the table and behind the door. I held my breath as he walked to the armchair and pushed it aside, but Nora wasn't there.

He turned to me. 'I'll find her, never fear. And when I do—' He huffed like a steam train and marched out of the room.

I waited a minute or two, then peeked outside. The corridor was empty.

'It's all right,' I whispered. 'You can come out. He's gone.'

But Nora did not reappear.

CHAPTER 11

'Nora, where are you?' I went from room to room, fighting the urge to call more loudly, but I didn't want to bring the superintendent back. Apart from him being unpleasant, that would definitely stop Nora returning. So I prowled, peeping behind curtains and under tables, but there was no sign of her.

'You can come out now, Nora,' I muttered. 'Superintendent Hicks left. I'm speaking the truth. If I wasn't, you'd know soon enough.'

Why was she so scared of him, anyway? Obviously he was very much senior to her, but Nora's reaction wasn't the awed respect of a junior member of staff. She genuinely seemed frightened of what he might do if he got hold of her.

Can he get hold of her, even? I remembered how Nora had tried to grip Jack's shoulders: her hands had gone straight through him. That made it more peculiar. I sighed, looked about me once more, and considered what to do.

What had we been discussing before the superintendent came? That was the worst of dealing with Nora. There were always interruptions: things to explain, or an obstacle or diversion, like the superintendent, or the horses, or – something.

A street directory. That was it. We'd been wondering what sort of businesses were in the area, and which might have used paper like that of the anonymous letter. I didn't need Nora to work on that.

'I don't know if you can hear me,' I said, feeling very silly indeed, 'but I'm going to the file room to look for a street directory. Maybe I'll see you there.'

Silence.

A minute later I was on my way, keeping my eyes open for any ghostly presences, but the place seemed deserted.

What did the superintendent do when he wasn't visiting the file room or terrorising Nora? And why was he at the Bridewell at all? What bothered him so much that he couldn't leave and enjoy whatever afterlife there was?

I reached the staircase which led to the basement and switched on my phone torch. It was much easier this time. I even remembered the hole when I got to the bottom of the stairs. *I'm getting to know the place*, I thought, and felt rather pleased. Then I remembered the police station was being sold off in less than a fortnight.

Much good that'll do you. I produced my ring of keys and opened the door. Now, where to begin?

I scanned the room and noticed a row of books propped on one of the filing cabinets. I walked over and switched my torch on again to read their spines. Finally I spied a Liverpool street directory from 1964.

I eased it out and riffled through it until I found Prescot Street. There was the police station, and next to it a greengrocer. A butcher's was there, too: presumably the one Tom Tinsley had worked at. But I found no sign of the Tinsleys' drapers shop and no chandler's belonging to Bill Cracknell.

Could the shops have been further away? I looked for them in adjacent streets, flicking back and forth in the directory, but neither showed up. I found a telephone directory, but there was no listing for a B or a W Cracknell anywhere near, nor any Tinsleys. *How odd that both should move.*

I found another directory from 1960. This time both shops were there, along with many other businesses I had noted four years later. Had any other business changed hands? I wasn't sure whether it was significant or not. Another three businesses had changed hands in the four years: a milliner had been replaced by a tailor, a grocer by a laboratory furnisher, and a 'dealer, misc.' by a pawnbroker. I made a note of all of them, just in case.

I checked the nearby businesses and on a fresh page of my notebook made a list of any that might use coarse paper to wrap goods. There were quite a few. I reached *Cracknell W, chandler*. What did a chandler do, anyway? The only chandler I'd heard of was the one in *Friends*. I looked at my phone, then realised that wouldn't work. 'Darn,' I said, aloud. However, the row of books yielded a well-thumbed dictionary.

Chandler, n.

A purveyor of household goods or a dealer in a specific form of goods (e.g. ship's chandler)

Household goods... *What would that involve? Soap, perhaps? Cleaning products?* I tried to imagine a house from the 1960s. It would have gas, of course, and surely electricity and running water, but would people still buy things like candles? At any rate, it was the sort of shop that might still wrap things in paper. And ship's goods – rope, nails, hooks? – could hurt the shopkeeper's hands, so he'd probably wear gloves...

You're clutching at straws, Steph.

What else can I do? I retorted, in my head. *Now shut up, I'm busy.* It was almost like having Nora there, except that my inner self-doubt answered back less.

I stood up and stretched, my back cracking after

bending over the small print. I left the books where they were in case I needed them again, locked up, and headed for the yard. It was time to test out Tasha's internet tip.

I entered the yard carefully, prepared for a rush of hooves, or at the very least a rush of air and the sickening feeling of being galloped through, but felt nothing untoward whatsoever.

Had Nora been spinning me a yarn? But she'd seemed genuinely frightened. What would be the point of fooling me when it stopped her doing what she wanted?

I walked to the iron staircase, ducked underneath, and checked my phone.

Two bars.

'Yes!' I punched the air. 'Thanks, Tash!' I unlocked the phone and typed in *Liverpool newspaper archive.* Less than a second later the screen was full of links. 'Oh, how wonderful,' I murmured, leaning against the brick wall and luxuriating in the rush of information. Now, how to get what I needed?

It was behind a paywall, of course, but I managed to sign up for a free trial and began to browse. My first search term was *Tinsley draper.*

The screen filled with results, mostly small advertisements about sales, bargains or very reasonable prices. My gaze snagged on one as I scrolled:

CLOSING DOWN SALE
Everything must go. Pre-Christmas bargains.
Tinsley & Son, Drapers, Prescot Street

The date of the advertisement was early December 1962. So they had shut up shop not long after Tom's death.

'How awful,' I muttered, feeling slightly nauseous. How must they have felt? True, Nora had said they never visited Tom, but still – to lose a son like that. I wondered where they had gone, and what became of the family.

This isn't helping the investigation. Resolutely, I clicked *New Search* and typed in *Cracknell chandler.*

I was faced with more advertisements, though fewer sales, and the notice of his shop's closure came later, in early 1963. He was selling the business with goods and goodwill, so presumably he'd left shopkeeping entirely.

I clicked on *New Search* again. *Bill Cracknell*, I typed.

The result wasn't what I had expected.

The first link on the list was *Bill Cracknell as Iago and Miss Susan Farringdon as Desdemona in the Liverpool City Players' production of Othello at St Michael's Church Hall.* I clicked on the link and a grainy black-and-white photograph appeared. The contrast wasn't good, but I could make out who was who. Either Miss Susan Farringdon was pretty tall, or Bill Cracknell was quite small. He wore a big hat with a feather, which threw a shadow over his face, but what I could see of him was nondescript.

I went back to the search results. *Review: A Midsummer Night's Dream.*

I clicked and another photograph loaded, captioned *Bill Cracknell as Puck and Walter Wainwright as Bottom.* They looked as if they were sharing a joke. The photo was a head-and-shoulders shot, but Bill's companion was at least a head taller and broad with it.

'Surely not,' I murmured. My head was spinning with possibilities, but of one thing I was sure.

I had found the small man, and possibly the big man too.

CHAPTER 12

I ran into the station. 'Nora? Nora! Where are you? Come out and show yourself.' I walked from room to room, calling. 'Come on, Nora. The superintendent can't hurt you while I'm here, can he?'

'I wouldn't be so sure.' I whipped round to see Superintendent Hicks, arms folded, feet firmly planted on the floor.

'With respect, sir, you're a ghost. What can you do?' I really didn't know. However, the question worked. He stepped back so that he took up less of the corridor.

'I used to run this place, you know,' he said, his tone conversational. 'In some ways, I still do.'

What did that involve? 'If you don't mind asking, sir, how come you're still here?'

'I wish I knew,' he said. 'I thought I did a good job. I improved policing, I raised the number of cases solved per month. But nobody's perfect, are they?' He smiled a rueful smile. 'It's nice to have a conversation for a change. It gets lonely.'

'You could talk to Nora.'

His face darkened immediately. 'If you knew what I do— Anyway, what is your business here?'

'I'm on duty, sir. I was sent by Inspector Farnsworth—'

'Farnsworth, eh?'

'Have you met him?'

'I've seen him,' said the superintendent. 'Not that he's seen me.'

'So that was after you—'

'Of course. I, er, took on my present position in 1965. Your inspector would have to be an old man now for me to have met him in the usual way. And so many people come through here.' He surveyed the empty station. 'Or used to.' He focused on me again. 'But that isn't what I meant. You've been poking around in the file room and the detective offices. None of the others do that. They just sit there reading magazines or novels, or staring into space. You' – he emphasised the word with a jab of his forefinger – 'are up to something.'

How much should I tell the superintendent? If he had worked at the station until 1965, he would have been a senior officer when our case was in progress. 'Nora and I—'

He snorted, but didn't speak.

'Nora and I are investigating the case of the four fingers.' It sounded ridiculous, put like that. 'The case Tom Tinsley was arrested for.'

I half-expected Superintendent Hicks to explode, but he looked at me enquiringly, as if trying to remember. 'Tom Tinsley . . . Tom Tinsley… Oh yes. Rum business. Never was sure about it, but no one else fitted the bill as well as he did. Circumstantial evidence.'

'What if it wasn't him?'

'Unfortunately, the case never got to trial. If he had been tried by a jury, perhaps they would have found him not guilty. We'll never know.'

'Is there anything you recall of the case beyond what's in the file, sir?'

Superintendent Hicks chuckled to himself. 'Have you any idea how many cases passed through this place in its heyday, Constable – what is your name?'

'Stephanie Sharpe. Steph for short.'

Another little snort. 'Well, Constable Steph-for-short, this may surprise you, but I didn't go into the minutiae of every little case. That's why I had inspectors, and sergeants, and constables, like yourself. People under them, too.'

'So were you the superintendent in 1962?' He nodded. 'How do you know Nora so well? Did you know her when she was alive?'

'Oh yes.' He nodded more slowly. 'I'll give you a

piece of advice, Constable Steph-for-short. Don't trust Nora.'

I decided to ignore that. 'You haven't seen her in the last half hour, have you?'

He studied me, and slowly the corner of his mouth curled up. 'Not as such, but I can tell you where you will find her. In fact, I'll take you there myself.'

We walked down the corridor together, and after perhaps half a minute I realised he was leading me to the file room. *Perhaps he overheard us talking earlier. He must know she can go into the file room.* But as we descended the stairs, the superintendent confidently, with me moving cautiously behind, I grew more and more uneasy.

The superintendent walked straight through the door of the file room. *Doesn't that hurt?* I remembered how I had felt when he passed through me. *I suppose he's used to it.* After all, if ghosts didn't do that they'd be trapped in one room for ever. I shivered, took out my keys, and unlocked the door for what seemed like the twentieth time that day.

The superintendent was waiting by a cabinet I hadn't opened yet. 'She'll be in here,' he said. 'Second drawer.'

My eyes narrowed. 'Do you mean she's hiding in the cabinet?'

'In a manner of speaking.' That lopsided smile again. 'You'll need a key.'

I searched the ring for a key small enough to fit the tarnished keyhole. The cabinet opened easily, as if it had been used more frequently than the others. A sheet of thin card at the front said *PERSONNEL RECORDS: CONFIDENTIAL. NOT TO BE OPENED BY ANYONE BELOW THE RANK OF INSPECTOR UNLESS A SIGNED SHEET IS PRESENTED.*

I stared at the faded, dogeared folders. 'What am I looking for?'

'Her last name's Norris,' said the superintendent. 'It's a slim file. Though not as slim as it could be.'

My finger searched through the names. Everett . . . Gardner . . . Harris . . . Jackson . . . Mansfield . . . Marston . . . McKeever . . . Nash . . . Norris. I pulled out a file more battered and dogeared than the rest.

'Open it, and you'll see what I mean.' The superintendent stepped back.

I took the file to the table and sat down. My stomach was in a tight knot.

NORRIS, Nora. Position: Matron.

I looked up at the superintendent. 'Matron?'

'Yes,' he replied. 'They look after any women who come in. Supervise them, bring food, that sort of thing.'

'But she told me she was a—'

He rocked on the balls of his feet. 'I daresay she did. She probably thinks she is. When I was a detective I found her in my office more than once, snooping.'

I turned the page.

DISCIPLINARY RECORD:

14th December 1917: found in the file room without good reason. Verbal warning given.

5th June 1918: discovered in a detective office going through documents. Written warning given.

3rd March 1919: apprehended in a detective office by Hicks. Second written warning.

13th June 1919: missing from duty, whereabouts unknown. Final written warning.

26th June 1919: Employee absent. Reason given: influenza

Received news of employee's death on 5th July 1919 (influenza).

At least the bit about the Spanish flu was true. I put my head in my hands. 'I – I don't know what to say.'

'You don't have to say anything, Constable,' said Superintendent Hicks. 'She tried it on all the time. Pinching a helmet from the cloakroom and walking round the neighbourhood as if she was on the beat. Standing at the front desk if the officer on duty took a break. It was almost a relief when she died, hard as it is to say. She was a nuisance and a distraction.' He grimaced. 'I didn't know she was still at the station until *I* died. By then she was waltzing around as if she owned the place.'

I pushed my chair back and stood up. 'I – I need air. It's stuffy in here.' My head was spinning. The woman who had bossed me about and pushed me into taking on this case was an impostor. I opened the door and stumbled out, missing the hole in the floor by centimetres. I barely looked where I was going. I only wanted to get outside, where I knew Nora wouldn't – couldn't – be.

A light drizzle was falling. I turned my face up to it, but it was annoying rather than soothing, so I retreated under the iron steps for shelter. The police radio clipped to my belt chirruped.

I stared at it, disconcerted. Who wanted to speak to me? Automatically, I unclipped it and answered.

'Constable Sharpe, this is Sergeant Doughty.' I could hear his anger even through the static. 'Close up the Bridewell, return to Erskine Street immediately and report to me on arrival. Over and out.'

Then my phone buzzed again and a message flashed up from an unknown number. *Best hurry, he's really cross. Tasha x*

I wiped my wet face with my jumper sleeve and walked slowly inside, feeling as if the bottom had dropped out of my world.

CHAPTER 13

As I walked into the office, all chatter stopped. The only noise was someone typing on their keyboard before that, too, went quiet. I felt as if I was playing a cowboy walking into a saloon. I expected someone to start whistling any minute.

Sergeant Doughty got up from his desk, keeping his eyes on me. 'I'll be in interview room one,' he said. As he approached me to leave the room, he gave me a wide berth. *I'm not contagious*, I thought. *Or am I?*

I went to my desk, out of habit, and put down the keys for the Bridewell.

'Hello, Steph,' said Sam, eventually. 'The sergeant's waiting.'

'Um, thanks. Do you know why—'

'He just said he wanted to see you.' Her face was expressionless.

I turned to go back out, and as I walked I heard a

couple of whispers behind me. By the time I opened the door, the noise had risen to a light hum. It seemed distant, as if it was happening to someone else. *What have I done? Will this go on my record? They can't sack me, can they?* And the worst of it was that I didn't know. Nothing in my training, or in *Blackstone's*, had prepared me for this.

I tapped on the door of interview room one. 'Enter,' said Sergeant Doughty.

I obeyed and closed the door, wondering what to say. In the end I settled for 'I got your message, sir.'

'Do you know why you're here?' Sergeant Doughty's face gave nothing away, but this wasn't unusual. He would have been an excellent poker player: perhaps he was. He delivered both praise and criticism in the same deadpan way, so it was hard to be sure which was which, or if he was being sarcastic. When I'd arrived Tasha had told me that Sergeant Doughty had a reputation for being a stickler. 'Dot your Is and cross your Ts,' she'd said, with a wary look around first, as if he might materialise behind her.

I considered how to reply. 'I just know that you asked me to come back, sir.'

'And you have no idea why.'

I had some idea, but I couldn't be sure what the sergeant knew already. 'I'm afraid I don't, sir.'

He studied me, without asking me to sit down.

'Really, Constable. Has it occurred to you that there is such a thing as the Data Protection Act?'

So it was the files. 'Yes, sir.'

'I happened to hear one of your colleagues mention a little investigation you have been conducting at the Bridewell.'

'Not an investigation as such—'

'Are you contradicting me?'

'No, sir. I was just—'

'Are you saying that you did not go into the file room at the Bridewell and read case files?'

'No, sir. I mean, no, I'm not saying that. I did go into the file room.' My face was burning hot.

'So you went snooping around, despite Constable Davies's instruction not to explore a largely unsafe building. You opened a locked door, and proceeded to open how many filing cabinets?'

I swallowed. 'One or two, sir.'

'One or two filing cabinets. Did you at any point seek permission to do this?'

I felt about ten centimetres tall. 'No, sir.'

'Did you take any files out of the cabinets?'

'Just one, sir.' I decided Nora's file could be left out of this, since I had no idea how to explain it.

'What happened then? I assume you opened the file and read the contents. Did you make notes?'

My notebook was heavy in my pocket. 'I did, sir.'

'Did you take either the file or those notes out of

the room?'

My heart was beating so loud that I was surprised he couldn't hear it. 'I did, sir. But the file is still at the station and the door is locked.'

'That's something.' Sergeant Doughty put his elbows on the table and made a staple of his fingers. 'May I ask why you disregarded the instructions you were given?'

I thought of all that had happened yesterday and today. Meeting Nora and investigating a proper case for the very first time, experiencing the thrill of piecing things together, and receiving what seemed like encouragement from Inspector Farnsworth. 'I heard about a case long ago which never went to trial, and I wondered if I could find out more.'

'So you went poking around where you shouldn't.' His tone was so flat that you could have ironed a shirt on it.

'I went to the file room.'

'That suggests you don't think that you shouldn't have gone there, Constable.'

I knew I was on shaky ground. 'I didn't receive a specific instruction not to go there, sir.'

'Oh, so it's Constable Davies's fault? Shall I call her in and tell her you're blaming her?'

'No, sir, I'm not blaming her.' I fought down the panic rising in my chest. Sergeant Doughty, if he wanted, could twist my words into anything. I was sure of it.

'Good.' Sergeant Doughty converted the steeple into tightly clasped hands, fingers interlaced. 'Constable Sharpe, I daresay you've noticed that I have not made notes on this conversation, which makes it an unofficial reprimand.'

My stomach unknotted itself a little. 'Yes, sir. Thank you, sir.'

'That does not mean that this is not a serious matter. It has been noted.' He unclasped his fingers and tapped the side of his head twice. 'If you like files so much, there is plenty of filing to be done here.'

My heart sank. 'Sir—'

He held up the finger he had tapped his head with. 'Please allow me to finish. If that does not suit you, there is always the option of being transferred back to your original post. That would of course require a full explanation to your senior officer.' He gave me a look that went right through me.

'I understand, sir. Sorry, sir.'

'Quite.' I fidgeted under his steady gaze. 'You do realise, Constable, that as you cannot be trusted to do your duty at the Bridewell, another officer will be posted there in your place. An officer who cannot be spared, given our current staffing levels and the amount of work we have to do.'

I blinked hard to stop myself from crying. 'I'm really sorry, sir. If you let me go back to the

Bridewell, I swear I'll stay in the main room and never enter the file room again.'

'Mmm.' The sergeant considered me. 'Is everything in good order at the Bridewell? Are the files put away as they should be? Have you left anything behind?'

I recalled Nora's personnel file. I couldn't remember whether I'd left it on the table. And I suspected Tom Tinsley's file was in the detective office upstairs. I bit my lip. 'I left my copy of *Blackstone's* there, sir. And *Police* magazine.'

The silence lengthened till I could scarcely bear it. 'In that case, I shall send someone to the Bridewell with you to, ah, collect your belongings. Once that is done, I expect to hear no more of this. Do you understand, Constable?'

'Yes, sir.'

'Good. Ask Constable Saunders to come here, please, and wait at your desk until she returns.'

'Thank you, sir.'

I marched out of the office, my jaw clenched so tight that it ached. Nora, with her half-truths and evasions, had caused this, and I was taking the blame. *This could be a serious setback to my career. Sergeant Doughty will never forget it.*

But you wanted to investigate, another voice argued in my head. *You could have refused to get involved, but you didn't.*

But if she hadn't told me about it—

So you have no mind of your own? What are you, a puppet?

That's not fair— 'Oof!' The air rushed out of my chest as I walked into something that shouldn't have been there. When I recovered my breath and looked up, it was Inspector Farnsworth.

'Oh sir, I'm so sorry, I—' *That's it*, I thought. *That's done it, for sure.* I could feel tears trying to surface and dug my nails into my palms in an effort to fight them down. I took a deep breath and turned away.

'Are you all right, Constable?' At least he sounded concerned rather than angry.

'Not really, sir,' I muttered, barely able to speak. 'I – expect you know what's happened. I won't try and justify it. I thought I was doing the right thing, but obviously I wasn't. Tasha – Constable Saunders – is taking me to get my things.'

I felt him take my arm. 'From the Bridewell?' His touch was very light.

I nodded.

'I've just been speaking to Constable Davies about it; she told me where you were. Don't disturb Constable Saunders, I'll accompany you.'

'But sir, Sergeant Doughty said—'

'I'll deal with the sergeant. Wait here.'

I watched, too stunned to react, as he strolled to the

interview room, knocked, put his head round the door, and exchanged a few words. He closed the door quietly and came back. 'I suggest you take a few moments to compose yourself before we set off.'

'You're not angry with me, sir?'

'Oh no.' He scrutinised me as if I was an interesting specimen under a microscope. 'I'm intrigued.'

CHAPTER 14

'Well,' said Inspector Farnsworth.

We had stopped on the way to the Bridewell to buy more milk, and I made us tea in the big room downstairs. I'd thought of suggesting we go to the detective office, as Nora and I had done most of our work on the case there, but it didn't feel right. Inspector Farnsworth had accepted a cup of tea – white, no sugar – and had merely said 'So.'

That opened the floodgates, and I told him the whole story, from Nora's unexpected appearance to the moment when her deception was revealed. It was a relief, like cleaning out a dusty old cupboard and making a pile of things to throw away. That made me pause. Should I put this behind me?

'I'm sorry,' I said. 'I'm probably talking far too much. It's all in the past, I suppose.'

Inspector Farnsworth sipped his tea and put his mug down. 'It is, but that doesn't stop it being important. Otherwise we wouldn't bother with history, would we? Justice isn't less important because time has passed.' He had a faraway look in his eyes. 'You actually saw these people? Nora, and Jack, and the superintendent?'

'Yes. I did.'

He glanced around the room. 'They aren't here now, are they?'

'No.' I couldn't help smiling. 'I would have mentioned.'

'Good.' He stood up and began to pace. 'I wonder...'

'Superintendent Hicks said he'd seen you.'

The inspector turned sharply. 'Did he? When?'

'He didn't say. I could ask him if he shows up, but the only time I know for sure where he is is at nine thirty when he goes to the file room. Nora told me.'

He regarded me. 'How do you feel about Nora?'

I shrugged. 'I don't know. She lied about who she was.'

'Was she a good colleague?'

I recalled the discoveries we'd made together. 'Mostly, yes. But she did odd things and she couldn't go in certain places. Because of the superintendent, or being scared of the horses.'

The inspector raised his eyebrows. 'Police horses?'

'Yes. Ghost ones. I never saw them.'

'I've never seen Nora, but that doesn't mean I don't

believe in her. But you haven't answered my question. How do you feel about Nora? Would you work with her again, knowing what you do now?'

'It explains a lot,' I said, slowly. 'If I hadn't found out she was just a matron, I wouldn't have known she wasn't a real officer. I've spent more time with her than any of my real colleagues at the station. She wanted to know the truth.' I paused. 'I'm talking about her as if she's dead – well, not here any more. I hope she hasn't gone. This is her home. Although if it's demolished—' I felt dizzy, and drank more tea to study myself.

'Where did you say you first met her? The detective office, wasn't it? Shall we go there?'

I stood up, and together we climbed the stairs to the offices. 'Nora!' I called. 'Nora, come out.' My voice was thin and echoey in the stairwell. I opened the door, half expecting to see Nora sitting in the armchair or bending over documents on the table, but the room was empty.

'It's been a while since I was up here,' said Inspector Farnsworth. He walked around the room, surveying its contents.

'Did you ever – see anything, Inspector?'

He moved the net curtain aside and peered out of the window. 'I felt something, definitely, but I was a busy young constable. Far too busy to think about what I felt, or want to take it further, when so many other things demanded my attention. Now, when I take a larger view of what justice is, and what it is to be a representative of the law, I'm busy managing my staff and dealing with matters of the present day.' He let the curtain fall and turned back to me. 'That probably sounds like an excuse. I would love to experience what you have, Steph, but I doubt I ever shall.'

I heard a scuffling noise and cocked my head. Where was it coming from?

'Perhaps I'm too old,' said the inspector. 'I don't know how these things work.'

The scuffling was coming from the fireplace. I walked towards it. 'Can you hear that?'

'Hear what?'

'Something's up the chimney. Maybe a bird's trapped, or—'

Nora landed in the grate and the rush of air made dust fly out at me. I sneezed, twice.

'Sorry,' said Nora. 'I was hiding because of the superintendent, and— Hello?' She got to her feet, watching the inspector, who was gaping at her, and brushed down her skirts. 'Can you see me?'

The inspector managed to close his mouth. 'I take it you're Nora,' he said, eventually.

'That's right,' said Nora. 'And from what I heard up there, you're an inspector. Pleased to meet you.' She held out a dusty hand, which the inspector stared at.

'You won't be able to shake it in the usual way,' I said. 'We did this.' I went through the motions.

'Ah,' said the inspector, and did the same with Nora.

'Nora,' I said, 'I found out you aren't a constable.'

'Was it the superintendent?' Nora looked resigned rather than angry.

'He led me to your personnel file.'

'So I might as well go.' Nora walked towards the open door.

'No, wait—' She turned. 'It doesn't matter. It shouldn't matter. We work well together.'

'Really?' Nora's grin lit up her face. 'I'm sorry I led you up the garden path, Steph. I didn't think you'd want anything to do with me if you knew the truth.'

'To be honest, if you'd told me the truth, I probably wouldn't have,' I said. 'So it's as well you didn't.'

Nora faced the inspector. 'I didn't lie, exactly—'

'Hmm,' I said. 'You definitely steered me the wrong way.'

Inspector Farnsworth held up his hands. 'We don't need to have this debate now, do we? There's a case to work on.'

'Oh yes,' said Nora. 'Absolutely. Don't you agree, Steph?'

I rolled my eyes, and nodded.

***

'So you think the short man was Bill Cracknell,' said the inspector. 'Who was the large man with him in the photograph?'

I frowned as I tried to remember. 'Something Wainwright. William Wainwright? Will Wainwright? I could return to the yard and find the photo—'

'Walter Wainwright?' asked the inspector.

'That's it! I knew it began with a W.' I stared at him. 'How did you know?'

Inspector Farnsworth laughed. 'Whispering Walter Wainwright is a local legend. Well before my time, but people still told the stories. He was a local bookie. He got a shop as soon as it became legal, but he'd worked out of the pubs for years – not that that was legal, but apparently the police turned a blind eye, because they liked a flutter too. He left the business when he made an absolute fortune on a boxing match. Tornado Tompkins, the northern welterweight champion, versus a complete unknown. No one expected the underdog to win, but he did, and everyone had bet on the Tornado. There were accusations of match rigging, but nothing was ever proved.'

'So he whispered,' said Nora. 'That would fit with what Jack said about the big man's husky voice.'

'Indeed it would,' said the inspector.

'But when did the fight take place?' I asked.

'Could it have anything to do with this?'

'We can soon find out.' The inspector held up his phone.

'We'll have to go into the yard,' I said. 'There's only one place where you can get a signal.'

Nora made a face. 'I'll see you in a few minutes. You and your calculators.'

'Why don't you come?' asked the inspector.

Her mouth remained turned down. 'Horses. Don't like 'em.'

'How about if we said we'd look after you?' he asked.

Nora considered this. 'I could try,' she said grudgingly.

'Come on.' The inspector went to the door, then paused. 'Steph, you'll have to show me the way. It's been so long that I've forgotten.'

We marched to the yard doorway and arranged ourselves in a Nora sandwich. 'Off we go,' said the inspector. 'Left, right, left, right…'

'I don't like this,' said Nora. 'They're looking at me.'

'Are they moving?' said the inspector.

'No, but they're thinking about it.'

'As long as they aren't moving, you're fine.'

'We're heading to the steps, Inspector,' I put in. 'Nora, why don't you go up them? The horses can't follow you there.'

'Oh yes!' Nora broke free and ran halfway up the steps, then leaned over the railings and shouted, 'Take that, stupid horses!'

'I suppose it's progress,' I said, and took the inspector to stand beneath her.

'Right,' said the inspector. 'Boxing match, Tornado, Liverpool.' He typed into his phone rapidly. 'Let's see what we get.' He peered at the screen. 'Shock defeat. That's promising,' he said, clicking a link.

'What's going on?' called Nora.

'3rd November 1962, Liverpool Stadium,' I called back. 'That fits! It could easily have something to do with the case.'

'What do we do now?' she replied.

The inspector and I looked at each other. 'I don't know,' he said. 'I hadn't thought that far.'

'What would we do if we could do anything?' I wasn't sure that was the right question to ask, but given how odd this all was, it sort of made sense to me.

'We'd ask Tom what happened,' said Nora.

'But how?' asked the inspector. 'Where would he be?'

'Well,' I said, my brain working furiously. 'Nora's still here because she has something she needs to do. So is the superintendent. Tom isn't here, so he could be—'

'At the jail!' cried Nora. She beamed as if she'd won the lottery. Then her face fell. 'Is it still there? I mean, *he* might be, but if the prison's been knocked down—'

'It's still there,' said the inspector. 'And so is someone who may be able to help us.'

I raised my eyebrows. 'Who?'

He smiled. 'You'll find out when we get there.'

CHAPTER 15

Nora squealed in the back seat of the police car. 'We're going so fast! Is this legal?'

'Nora, we're crawling,' I said. 'We're doing twenty.' I turned to look at her. The joy on her face was infectious, and I grinned. 'I'm glad you're enjoying it.'

'I didn't think I'd be able to leave the Bridewell,' said Nora. 'And here I am, in a real-life police car, investigating a case!' She chuckled and rubbed her hands together. 'How far is it now, Inspector?'

'About a mile less than the last time you asked,' said Inspector Farnsworth. But he was smiling too.

It had caused quite a stir when the inspector and I went to Erskine Street station to announce that he was visiting HMP Liverpool.

'That isn't in the diary, sir,' said Sergeant Doughty.

'No, it isn't,' said the inspector. 'Something came up. And Constable Sharpe is accompanying me.'

Sergeant Doughty regarded me as if I was a piece of chewing gum on his shoe. 'Really, sir? Is that wise, given her recent conduct?'

Inspector Farnsworth grinned. 'That's why she's coming with me, Trevor. I'll be taking a car. Expect me when you see me.' I longed to give Sergeant Doughty a cheeky look, but I kept my gaze on the inspector's back as I followed him out of the room. Who knew what would happen next? Would Tom even be there?

Inspector Farnsworth pulled up at a red light outside the Valley pub. 'Not too far now we're out of city traffic,' he said. 'Have you visited the prison before, Steph?'

'No,' I said, shaken out of my thoughts. 'I've only been here a week or so.'

'Oh. In that case—' The lights changed and we moved forward.

'Can we go faster?' asked Nora.

'Not without putting the blues and twos on,' said the inspector. 'Lights and sirens,' he added, for her benefit.

'Can we?'

'I don't think it's necessary,' said the inspector. 'Apart from anything else, we should keep our presence low-key.'

We continued down surprisingly quiet roads, then turned right at a roundabout. 'Almost there,' said the inspector. He slowed and indicated left.

This can't be right, I thought, gazing at the long, low, modern building. The complex was much bigger than that of the women's prison I had occasionally driven past in my previous job. Then I saw a red-brick building behind the main building. With small tower-like pillars at each corner and cross-shaped windows on its top floor, it was more like a small castle than a prison. Even the car park was a bit daunting.

'Here we are,' said the inspector, gathering his belongings from the central compartment. 'I assume you have a notebook, Constable.'

'Of course,' I said, patting my pocket. We got out and closed the doors, but Nora remained inside the car. I opened her door, but she still sat there. 'Come along, Nora.'

She looked at me, her face a picture of misery. 'I've never been in a prison before. Will I be all right?'

'I assume so,' I said. 'Strangely, they didn't cover it in Police 101.'

She looked at me, wide-eyed. 'Didn't they?'

I laughed. 'It's just an expression. You should be fine. It's not as if most people will be able to see you.'

She brightened a little. 'That's true.' She scrambled out of the car and hurried towards the doors. 'Come on, we haven't got all day.'

The inspector and I exchanged glances and

followed her.

We entered the reception and approached the member of staff on duty, who was behind a layer of glass. 'Good afternoon,' said the inspector, showing his warrant card. 'Inspector Farnsworth from Merseyside Police, and this is my colleague Constable Sharpe. I'd like a word with Mr Fagan.'

The member of staff seemed puzzled. 'Mr Fagan? Is that a new prisoner?'

'No, one of your team. You'll know him better as Lucy.'

Now it was my turn to be puzzled. *Lucy?*

The man laughed. 'Oh, Lucy! You should have said.' He picked up his phone and dialled a number. 'Pat? Ask Lucy to come to the front desk, would you. I've got an inspector who wants him.' He listened for a moment, then put the phone down. 'He'll be here in a jiffy. Sign in, both of you. Put your tech and any prohibited items into this bag, and I'll let you into the airlock.'

We did as we were told, apart from Nora, and a buzzer sounded. 'Push the door,' said the man, and we walked into a space the size of a large lift. There were notices on the board concerning prohibited items and acceptable conduct. I was starting to get claustrophobic when the door on the other side opened and we saw an elderly man with a white ponytail, wearing a prison officer's uniform.

113

'Inspector Farnsworth,' he said. 'This is a surprise.'

'Adam,' said the inspector. 'Always a pleasure.'

'Come this way,' said Adam.

'I'd like to ask you about a former prisoner of yours,' said the inspector, as we walked. 'A man called—'

'Let's wait until we are in my sanctum,' said Adam. 'All in good time.' Nora looked extremely worried.

'Can I ask a question?' I asked. 'Why did the man on duty call you Lucy?'

Adam chortled. 'I am, among other things, the prison archivist and historian. Lucy is short for Lucy Worsley. Before she was on TV, they used to call me Starkey. After David.'

'Oh, I see!' I giggled.

'And who might you be?' His brown eyes seemed to look right into me.

'Constable Stephanie Sharpe,' I replied, fighting the urge to straighten up. I took out my warrant card and showed it to him.

He held out a thin, pale hand. 'Delighted to meet you.' He shook my hand gravely. 'And your companion?'

Nora gasped. 'You can see me?'

'I can,' said Adam. 'I see a lot.' He considered her. '1920ish? Matron?'

'Nora Norris.' Nora did a little curtsey. 'I've never been noticed by so many people in one day. Not even when I was alive.'

Adam led us outside, and soon we were standing before the forbidding, castle-like building I'd seen on our way in. 'Admin block,' he said. He opened the door and let us pass in, then closed it behind us. I followed the inspector down various corridors, so conscious of Nora gazing around apprehensively that I barely took in a thing.

'Welcome to my lair,' said Adam, stopping at a door marked *Archive*. 'I'm afraid I can't offer you refreshment, because of the ledgers. I have to be strict about these things.'

The room was small and windowless, and lined from floor to ceiling with shelves crammed with leather-bound books. 'What are we looking for?' asked Adam.

'A young man called Tom Tinsley,' said Inspector Farnsworth. 'He came to you in early November 1962. He wasn't with you long.'

'1962...' Adam's bony finger ran along the shelves and he drew out a book. 'Let me see.' He opened the book flat on the plain wood table in the middle of the room and leafed carefully through the pages. 'Ah yes. He arrived on the fifth of November and was put into solitary confinement in— Oh, how interesting.'

'What is?' I asked.

'He was put in a cell on H wing: H27. That cell isn't used any more: everyone who spends more than ten minutes in it feels uneasy and asks to move.'

'How odd,' said the inspector. 'Since when?'

'Since even before I came to the prison,' said Adam. 'So that would fit with your timeline.'

'Could we visit the cell?'

Adam regarded the inspector keenly. 'You can, as H wing is currently closed for refurbishment.' He continued to watch the inspector. 'What is your object?'

'We wish to speak to Tom, if possible. We are investigating his case.'

I half-expected Adam to burst out laughing and escort us back to the airlock, but he closed the ledger and replaced it on the shelf. 'I'll see what I can do.'

Adam took us through the admin block and into the main prison. I sensed Nora trembling beside me as we walked. Then he produced a ring of keys. 'Welcome to H Wing.'

We entered a dark, echoing space and I heard Nora gasp. When the lights came on, we saw tins of paint and neatly stacked cardboard boxes. It reminded me a little of the Bridewell, till I looked past the boxes to the metal walkways and staircases leading to what seemed like hundreds of cells.

Adam moved towards the left-hand side of the huge room. 'Now,' he said, walking slowly, 'H27 . . .

ah, yes.' He stopped in front of a door identical to the others, and the ring of keys came out again. 'It's been a while since anyone was in here,' he said. 'It might take a bit of persuading.' The key turned, and the sharp click made me jump. 'Do you want me to come in, Inspector, or would you rather I stayed outside?'

'Please let him come in, Inspector,' whispered Nora. 'Tom could be very angry.'

'I wouldn't blame him,' said Inspector Farnsworth. 'Very well. Although if Tom won't talk, we may have to reconsider.' He took a deep breath, opened the door and walked in. I followed, my heart in my mouth, then Adam, and Nora brought up the rear.

It took my eyes a while to get used to the darkness. If the cell had ever been lit, it wasn't now.

'Tom?' I whispered. 'Tom Tinsley, are you there?'

'He's in the corner,' whispered Nora. 'I can feel it.'

I took a step forward to where she pointed, and the air grew colder. The further I advanced, the colder it became. 'Tom,' I said, addressing a point a little above my head, 'we've come to talk to you.'

'You're looking in the wrong place,' said Nora. 'He's sitting down.'

A faint glow brightened and sharpened until it became the shape of a fair-haired young man, his arms around his knees, gazing warily at us. He wore a prison uniform, and appeared to have been in a fight. I remembered the words from his file – *dashed himself against the walls of his cell* – and shuddered.

'I won't hurt you,' I said. 'I promise.'

'Like to see you try.' His voice was rough, as if he hadn't used it for some time. Possibly for years.

CHAPTER 16

'He's so young,' whispered Nora. 'I'd forgotten how young he was.'

Tom raised his head. 'I can hear you, you know. Even if I can't see you too well.'

'Sorry,' said Nora. 'I'm not sure who can see and hear me and who can't.'

'I know what that feels like,' said Tom. 'Anyway, I'm not so young. I'll be nineteen next birthday. Well, I would have been.'

Inspector Farnsworth crouched down. 'Hello, Tom. My name is Inspector Farnsworth – Frank, if you prefer – and I'd like to talk to you.'

'Don't know nothing,' said Tom, and buried his face in his knees.

'Can I try?' whispered Nora.

Inspector Farnsworth stood up and shrugged. 'Why not.'

Nora sat down near Tom and gradually moved

closer.

He peered at her suspiciously. 'What are you up to? And why are you dressed like that? You look like something out of a silent movie.'

'That's because I died in 1919,' said Nora.

'Oh.' But Tom continued to watch her.

'What the inspector's trying to say,' Nora continued, 'is that we don't think you did what you're supposed to have done. What you were locked up for.'

Tom's mouth twisted. 'Well, that's nice, but what does it matter? What's done is done.'

'Not necessarily,' said Inspector Farnsworth. 'I mean, you're stuck here, and that can't be much fun.'

Tom rested his chin on his knees. 'It isn't,' he said, very low. 'At least I get peace and quiet now. Some people carry on shocking.'

The inspector smiled. 'I do. So if we could get you unstuck somehow, would you like that?'

'You bet I would!' Tom grinned, and I could see the boy in him.

'Let's talk, then,' said Nora. 'How come you were waving a knife around in a back alley? That doesn't seem like you.'

Tom rounded on her. 'What would you know about me?'

Nora raised her hand and was about to put it on Tom's, then remembered and made a vague gesture. 'I recall you coming into the police station after I died.

You seemed a nice boy. Not the sort to cut fingers off, or threaten people with a knife.'

'I wasn't! I wasn't threatening people.' Tom looked at us all. 'I was practising.' His voice sunk lower. 'I swore not to tell, but I guess it doesn't matter now.'

'What were you practising, Tom?' I asked. 'And who made you promise not to tell?'

'It was for a play,' said Tom. '*The Lamentable Tragedy of Julius Caesar*. They told me the man who was meant to play Brutus had come down with shingles and wouldn't be fit to do it. They said I was to practise the stabbing scene with a knife, and gave me the lines to say. Not many, because my memory isn't good. They promised they'd take me to show the director, and if I got it right he'd be so impressed he'd hire me on the spot. But I was took up, and – you know the rest.'

'Oh, you poor boy.' Nora blinked hard and sniffed twice. 'So how did this come about?'

'Should we be asking—' I began, but Nora gave me a look that said *Keep out of it* more plainly than words.

'I was taking a walk after work one night,' said Tom. 'It was a nice evening, and I didn't feel like going home yet – too much noise – and I wasn't in the mood for the pub. So I was strolling along minding my own business, and as I was cutting down the back of the convent I heard a voice. A man talking, which I wasn't expecting, and he sounded like he had a sore throat. "So you take the money to the Tornado and tell him to go down in the third," he said.

"Are you sure of him?" said the other man, and I near jumped out of my skin, for it was Bill Cracknell. He had a very distinct way of speaking – a carrying voice. I'd seen him in the shows the drama group put on at Christmas and other times, and I'd have known him anywhere.

"Sure I'm sure," said the other man.

"Someone's here," said Bill, "I can sense it." That gave me a shiver, like I was at a play and something was going to happen. "Come out, whoever you are," he shouted, and I couldn't help myself.

I walked forward and took off my cap. "Good evening, Bill," I said. I couldn't see who the other man was, as they were both muffled to the eyebrows, but I knew Bill. He ran the chandler's shop, and he sold all sorts of other stuff which he kept under the counter. He was the pub darts champion, too, as well as doing the acting. Everyone knew Bill.

Bill muttered to his friend, then pulled his scarf down and smiled at me. "Now, young Tom, you've caught us rehearsing!"

"Rehearsing?" says I. "What for?"

"A play, of course," says Bill, with a big grin on his face. "*The Lamentable Tragedy of Julius Caesar*. But you can't tell anyone. It's a secret." His friend sniggered and he gave him a dig in the ribs. "In fact – stand up straight, will you?"

I did as I was told and Bill walked slowly around me. "It's a blessing we met you, young Tom," he said. "How would you like to be in the play?"

"Me?" I gasped. "No one's ever asked me to be in anything before, let alone a play."

"Yes, you. You're a fine strapping lad, exactly what we need." He took me aside and started to explain what he wanted. Then all of a sudden he looked doubtful and said he wasn't sure I could do it, but I insisted I could, and I'd practise, and I'd surprise him.

"All right," Bill said. "You get practising somewhere nice and quiet – lots of room in the alleys – and meet me here in a week to show me. Not a word to anyone, though, or the surprise will be ruined." He walked off whistling and I was alone, for the other man had disappeared while we were talking.'

'Can you remember when this happened?' I asked.

Tom frowned, thinking. 'Not the date. I never was good at dates, always forgot Ma's birthday. I reckon it was a Thursday. Yes, I'm sure. I had that sort of hopeful feeling you get on a Thursday, when you're over halfway and you've just got Friday and Saturday left to work.'

'We can check the date when I get my phone back,'

said Inspector Farnsworth.

'Yes,' I replied. 'From what I recall, Bill brought the box of fingers in on a Monday.'

A sort of strangled noise came out of Tom. 'Bill brought it in? *Bill* brought it?' He jumped to his feet.

'I'm afraid so,' said the inspector.

'Why, the— Was it him who said it was me?'

'No,' said the inspector. 'People had seen you brandishing a knife in the alley. And an anonymous letter pointed the finger at you.'

Written on paper which might have come from Bill's shop, I thought, but I kept it to myself.

'Oh,' said Tom, looking abashed. 'So what happened with the play? Did someone else play Brutus?'

'I haven't checked yet,' said the inspector, 'but I'm not sure there ever was a play. I think you were tricked.'

Tom's hands clenched into fists. 'That's mean. But why? Was Bill making fun of me, and it went wrong?'

'I'm afraid it's worse than that,' said Nora. 'You overheard them talking about fixing a big boxing match, and they framed you to get you out of the way. I'm sorry, Tom.'

Tom stared at her, horrified, then buried his head in his knees again and sobbed.

'What happens now?' I whispered to Inspector Farnsworth.

'I wish I knew,' he whispered back, his face a mask of worry. 'I was so focused on solving the case that I didn't think about what came after.'

'People never do,' said Nora, bitterly.

Adam shuffled forward. 'Some do. What are the names of this pair?'

'Bill Cracknell and Walter Wainwright,' I said. 'Not that it matters. All we've done is tell Tom what we know. We can't punish them.'

'No, we can't,' said Adam. 'But if I can remember the words...' He turned away for a moment, muttering to himself, then faced us and raised a hand. 'Bill Cracknell, you are wanted for questioning. Show yourself!'

Nothing happened. I let out a slow sigh of relief. I wasn't sure I could cope with any more—

The rush of air took everyone aback. It came from all around us, moving to the centre of the cell, and slowly the air thickened into a shape. The stooped shape of an old man, wearing a pale-blue polo shirt and chinos. Most of his hair had fallen out and he was deeply tanned, but I could still recognise a much older version of the man I had seen in the grainy black-and-white photos.

'What's all this?' asked Bill. His voice rang out, echoing around the cell. 'Who brought me here? What do you want?' His gaze fell on Tom, huddled on the floor, watching him. Bill's lip curled, and he was silent.

'Golly,' whispered Nora.

Adam looked at his hand as though he didn't trust it, then raised it again. 'Walter Wainwright, you are wanted for questioning. Sh—'

A larger form began to materialise, and as it filled out it knocked Bill aside. ''Ere, watch it,' said Bill.

'Sorry,' the figure croaked, and resolved itself into a large man in suit trousers and a black polo neck. He peered at Bill. 'Is that you, Bill?'

'It is, Walter,' said Bill. 'I've no idea what I'm doing here, and I daresay you haven't either.'

But Walter was staring at Tom. 'Is he that young lad? The one you stitched up all them years ago?'

Bill's gaze darted from one to the other of us, then back to Walter. 'What? Don't know what you mean, Walter. Think you're misremembering.' He tried to poke the other man in the chest, and failed.

'I forgot about it,' said Walter. 'I was busy working on the Tornado to throw that match, and you was doing the running for me so folks wouldn't link us. I thought you was joking about them fingers till I heard the tale in the pub.'

Bill eyed me, since I was the only one in a recognisable police uniform. 'Careful, Walter. I don't know how we got here, but I don't like it.' He spoke as if he wasn't sure if we could hear him or not.

'I don't suppose you do,' said Inspector

Farnsworth, 'but I suspect that you're stuck here until you admit what you did.'

A laugh bubbled out of Bill. 'What you going to do? Hang me? I'm dead already!' He winked at Walter. 'You can pour your heart out all you like and it won't make a lick of difference. Not to us, nor to that snivelling lump.' He faced us. 'All right, if a confession's what you want. The big match between the Tornado and Whatsisname Smith was rigged and I was the go-between. That's Walter's problem, not mine – I only did what I was told. As for the fingers, I got them from a friend at the hospital mortuary. No living people were harmed in the making of this prank – isn't that what they say? And a good joke for Halloween, too.'

'But why did you do it?' asked the inspector.

'We didn't trust Tom here not to talk about what he'd heard. I figured a few days cooling his heels at the Bridewell wouldn't hurt him, and would do us a lot of good. And yes, I wrote the anonymous note, as you lot were too incompetent to arrest him by yourselves.' He jerked a thumb at Tom. 'Anyone could see he didn't have the guts to do it, anyway.'

'Shut up, Bill!' Tom jumped to his feet. 'I've got guts, but I'd never do a thing like that.'

Bill laughed. 'Don't you tell me to shut up, young whippersnapper. What are you going to do, walk through me? *You* can't hurt me, Tom Tinsley. No one

127

can.' He thrust his chest out. 'No one can touch me.'

'*REALLY?*'

A new voice echoed around the cell, so deep that it made the floor vibrate.

Nora cast a panicked glance at Adam. 'How did you do that?'

Adam looked bewildered. 'I didn't.'

'*WILLIAM CRACKNELL*,' the voice intoned, '*YOU STAND CONDEMNED OUT OF YOUR OWN MOUTH. YOU MAY HAVE EVADED PUNISHMENT IN LIFE, BUT IT IS NEVER TOO LATE. YOU ARE GUILTY, AND THERE WILL BE NO APPEAL AGAINST THE VERDICT.*'

Bill whimpered. 'I didn't mean—'

'*OR THE SENTENCE.*'

All the colour drained out of his face. 'Stop it! You're choking me. You're choking me! I'll come quietly, I will...' He and his voice faded until there was nothing left of him.

Walter swallowed. 'I guess it's me next.'

'*YES*,' said the voice. '*YOU ARE REQUIRED TO TESTIFY, WALTER WAINWRIGHT. YOU WILL TELL THE TRUTH, THE WHOLE TRUTH, AND NOTHING BUT THE TRUTH.*'

'So help me,' whispered Walter, trembling. 'You won't do the squeezing thing on me, will you?'

'*COME NOW*,' said the voice, and Walter vanished so quickly that it seemed as if someone had switched him off.

We looked at each other, eyes wide, and no one spoke for what felt like several minutes.

'Has it gone?' whispered Nora.

We waited, but no boom answered her.

We sighed with relief. 'Thank you,' said Tom. 'I don't know who you are, except they call him Lucy.' He jerked a thumb at Adam. 'I've sat here wondering for I don't know how long. Wondering why. Wondering what I did to deserve it. Wondering whether I'd been bad.' He sighed. 'Now I see I was just in the wrong place at the wrong time, and too daft to know it.'

'I'm really sorry, Tom,' said Nora. 'You didn't deserve it. They were bad men, and they'll be judged properly.'

'Yes. I can stop worrying— Hello, what's this?' He held up his hand, which was even fainter than before.

'Tom, you're going to your rest.' Nora moved towards him. 'I'd hold your hand, but I can't.'

'It feels funny,' said Tom, but he was smiling as he faded. 'Tickly. No, tingly. As if—' And he was gone.

I turned to Inspector Farnsworth, who was staring at the space where Tom had been. 'It's odd, isn't it?' I said. 'That's what happened when Jack went to his rest, too.'

Inspector Farnsworth bowed his head for a moment. 'He looked happy,' he said. 'I suppose that

129

makes it a happy ending.'

'And we solved the case!' exclaimed Nora, beaming. 'We solved the case, and we brought them to justice, and Tom's at peace. So everything's good.'

'And I have one prisoner less to account for,' said Adam. 'You'd be amazed how many prisoners in here aren't on the official roll.'

'Lots to do, then,' said Nora, rubbing her hands.

'Perhaps,' said Inspector Farnsworth. 'But not today.'

I gazed around the dark cell where Tom Tinsley had spent his last days. *If only someone had persisted with him. If only his parents had visited, or the prison doctor had got through to him...*

I imagined all the other ghosts who must inhabit the prison. What stories did they have to tell? But then I yawned, and realised how tired I was.

'I agree with the inspector,' I said. 'Not today.'

CHAPTER 17

I finished going through my emails and shut down my computer.

'Off to the Bridewell again, Steph?' said Sam. She looked rather guilty. 'I'm sorry it's been dumped on you. I know someone's got to do it, but it's no fun.'

'I'll cope,' I said. 'At least it's quieter than this place.'

As if it had heard me, Sam's phone trilled. She snatched it up. 'Good morning, Constable Davies speaking.' She covered the mouthpiece with her hand, rolled her eyes, and mouthed *See you later.*

'It won't be for much longer, will it?' asked Tasha. 'I thought they were getting rid of the place.'

'You thought wrong,' said Huw as he breezed in, throwing a file on his desk. 'Apparently there's doubt about the structural integrity of the building, as if any of us couldn't have told them that. So the developers have pulled out, and I guess we're stuck with it.' He made a face. 'Sorry, Steph. Looks like you're there for the foreseeable.'

'It's OK,' I said, putting my coat on. 'It's good thinking time.' I opened my drawer for the keys and found a Snickers bar underneath them. Tasha gave me a shy smile and I smiled back. 'There's lots of paperwork to go through, anyway.' A snort came from the corner where Sergeant Doughty sat. 'See you later, maybe,' I said, and set off.

It was properly cold out now, and the morning frost hadn't melted yet. I stomped along Prescot Street, avoiding slippery patches, and let myself in. 'Hello,' I called. 'It's me.' I went through to the main room, switched the kettle on, and opened the mini fridge for some milk.

The days following our visit to HMP Liverpool had felt full of incident. Our first task had been to see if Tom Tinsley had any living family. Eventually, after tracing a path from the closing-down sale of Tinsley's drapers, we found that the Tinsleys had emigrated to Australia.

Inspector Farnsworth set up a Zoom call with them, with the Sydney police supporting at the other end. Tom's parents were long gone, of course, but we spoke to his younger sister Millie and his niece and nephew.

'It's such a relief,' said Millie. 'Ma and Pa thought that by emigrating we could start again, but something like that never leaves you. You always worry someone will find out.' She dabbed at her eyes with a tissue. 'I wish we could tell Ma and Pa.'

Tom can pass it on himself, I thought. The inspector gave me a warning look, then transferred it to Nora, who was sitting out of range of the camera, just in case.

The media had also picked up the story. *MISCARRIAGE OF JUSTICE,* read the headline on the *Echo. Police solve cold case and unravel the mystery of the Tornado Tompkins defeat.* They were far more interested in the boxing match than Tom's wrongful conviction.

The public voiced two main opinions. Sports fans argued that the Tornado's titles should not stand, and neither should that of the man who had unexpectedly defeated him. Several people also wrote to the paper or posted on social media, demanding to know why the police were investigating crimes in the previous century when there was more than enough to do in the present.

'I should have expected it,' said Inspector Farnsworth. 'People are obsessed with the present.'

'Well, yes,' said Nora. 'It's all we have.'

I looked at her, surprised. 'That's deep.'

Nora shrugged. 'Lots of thinking time.'

Where is Nora this morning? I thought, as I made tea. I recalled the events of the previous afternoon, when we had finally crossed the last T and dotted the last I. The paperwork had been completed, the file updated, and the case closed.

'What now?' I had asked Inspector Farnsworth.

'Good question,' he replied. 'There is plenty to do here. If I could…' He gazed around him sorrowfully. 'My work at Erskine Street is a full-time job, though. More than that.'

'I could stay and keep things going,' I said. 'I wouldn't mind.'

'I hoped you'd say that.' He smiled at me. 'You'll have to keep what you're doing quiet, though. Nora, how about you?'

'Try and stop me,' said Nora. 'There's just one thing…'

'Oh yes? What's that?'

'I don't suppose you have matrons any more. In any case, I'm not doing a matron's job now.'

'Good point,' said the inspector. 'Steph, may I borrow a page of your notebook, please?'

My eyebrows were halfway up my head, but I passed over my notebook.

The inspector took a pen from his inner jacket pocket. *TO WHOM IT MAY CONCERN*, he wrote, and underlined it. *I hereby appoint Nora Norris as an acting constable in the Merseyside Police. Inspector F Farnsworth.* He ripped the sheet out and showed it to Nora. 'Will that do?'

'Do?' Nora's face was bright red. '*Do?*' She did a little jig on the spot. 'If I could, I'd hug you, Inspector!'

'Um, well—' The inspector fiddled with his pen.

Nora shot me a look. 'Steph, would you take care of that for me?'

'Of course.' I took the sheet from the inspector, folded it, and tucked it inside the cover of my notebook. I could have sworn that Nora's eyes were wet with tears if I hadn't known that was impossible.

And now I was worried. 'Nora?' I took my mug and wandered around the station. 'Nora?'

But I couldn't see Nora anywhere. I was so concerned that I went to the file room at nine thirty-five and intercepted Superintendent Hicks. 'Have you seen Nora, sir?'

Inspector Hicks was busy reading the newspaper I had left on the table, its pages open to the story about the Tom Tinsley case. 'What? Oh, it's you.'

'Have you seen Nora?' I repeated. 'I haven't, and I'm a bit worried. She was so happy yesterday, and I'm wondering if she's . . . she's—'

'Gone to her rest?' The superintendent laughed. 'I'm afraid you're not rid of her yet. I saw her not five minutes ago, out in the yard facing down the horses.'

'Thank you!' I made for the door.

'Wait a minute, young what's-your-name.' He tapped the newspaper with his forefinger, though it made no sound. 'You did well. You and this inspector . . . and Nora, I suppose.' He coughed her name out like a fishbone.

'We couldn't have done it without her,' I said. 'I'll go and find her.'

Just as the superintendent had said, Nora was in the yard. What he hadn't mentioned was that she was stretching out her hand to a large chestnut horse, which was sniffing it curiously. 'I'd love to give you a sugar lump,' she told it, 'but I don't think there's such a thing as ghost sugar.'

I laughed. 'I didn't think there were such things as ghost horses, and here we are.'

Nora giggled. 'True.'

'So you're not scared of horses any more?'

Nora shook her head. 'It was silly, really. I was frightened by a horse when I was a little girl, and I always worried that one would come after me and hurt me. But there isn't much one could do to me now, is there? Except run through me, and that's only uncomfortable for a second or two.'

I walked over to her. 'I was worried you might have...'

Nora gave me a sharp look. 'Might have what?'

'You know.'

'Oh, you mean like Tom? I might have done what I needed to go to my rest?'

I nodded, not wanting to say yes in case it triggered

136

something. 'I thought – what with solving your first case, and Inspector Farnsworth making you a constable—'

Nora burst out laughing. 'You thought that was enough? Believe me, Steph, I've only just begun! Think of what you and I could do together – the cases we'll solve and the criminals we'll bring to justice when they least expect it! With the inspector's help, of course,' she added.

'Of course,' I said, feeling rather overwhelmed, and drained my mug of tea.

WHAT TO READ NEXT

Steph and Nora's next investigation is *The Case of the Haunted Ghost*.

When the duo are sent to investigate a poltergeist wreaking havoc at a prestigious members' club in Liverpool, they assume it'll be easy. It turns out to be anything but.

Nora's former boss, Superintendent Hicks, is the only one who can see the ghost at first – and he's far from pleased when he recognises him. The ghost himself, a club member until very recently, is horrified by the presence of another invisible spirit who is most definitely not a member. He doesn't know why he feels such revulsion – and he won't cease his mischief until the offending spirit is removed.

Worse still, Nora begins to realise what she has missed out on in life, and fears that her position in the team is under threat. What will she do if her vocation is taken away?

Take a look at *The Case of the Haunted Ghost* here: https://mybook.to/SpiritLaw2 (global link).

If you enjoy light mystery with more than a touch of magic, you might enjoy my *Magical Bookshop* series. The first book is *Every Trick in the Book*, and can be found at http://mybook.to/bookshop1 (global link).

If you liked the creepy, spooky nature of this book, you might enjoy my series of *Halloween Sherlock* novelettes, which are fairly traditional in nature and have a similar atmosphere. The first in series is *The Case of the Snow-White Lady:* http://mybook.to/SnowWhiteLady (global link).

However, if you prefer contemporary mysteries in a village setting, you could try the *Booker & Fitch Mysteries* (written with Paula Harmon) or the *Pippa Parker Mysteries.*

The first Booker and Fitch book is *Murder for Beginners*: http://mybook.to/Beginners (global link).

The first Pippa book is *Murder at the Playgroup* (don't worry, no children are harmed!): http://mybook.to/playgroup (global link).

ACKNOWLEDGEMENTS

As ever, my first thanks go to my wonderful and very speedy beta readers – Carol Bissett, Ruth Cunliffe, Paula Harmon, and Stephen Lenhardt. Thank you so much for your feedback and suggestions! Any errors that remain are mine only.

This book was a happy accident. In mid-September I booked a tour of the Bridewell Studios and Gallery on a Heritage Open Day (https://www.heritageopendays.org.uk). There I learnt about the building's history as a former police station, saw the cells, heard that a box of fingers was once brought there, and found out that the building is reputed to be haunted... I mean, how could I let all that pass? So many thanks are due to Fiona Filby, our tour guide! If you would like to know more about the Bridewell and its new life as artists' studios and a cultural space, do visit https://www.bridewellstudiosliverpool.org.

I thought I would write a one-off short story about

the Bridewell, like my Halloween Sherlock mysteries. However, being me, as I plotted the idea grew and grew until it became a novella – and here it is.

A quick disclaimer: while the Bridewell is a former police station, the Merseyside Police officers and the other characters depicted in the book are not based on any from real life. Erskine Street Police Station is fictional, and while HMP Liverpool is real, its depiction in this book is fictitious.

And finally, many thanks to you, the reader. I hope you've enjoyed this book. If you have, please consider leaving a short review or rating on Amazon and/or Goodreads. Reviews and ratings are hugely important to authors, as they help books find new readers.

COVER CREDITS

Image (rotated, scaled up, altered in brightness): 'On Cobbled Lanes' by Pete: https://www.flickr.com/photos/23408922@N07/30376608113. Shared under Creative Commons license 2.0: https://creativecommons.org/licenses/by/2.0/.

Cover font: IM FELL Great Primer Pro by Igino Marini: https://www.fontsquirrel.com/fonts/im-fell-great-primer-pro. License: SIL Open Font License v1.10: https://www.fontsquirrel.com/license/im-fell-great-primer-pro.

ABOUT THE AUTHOR

Liz Hedgecock grew up in London, England, did an English degree, and then took forever to start writing. After several years working in the National Health Service, some short stories crept into the world. A few even won prizes. Then the stories started to grow longer...

Now Liz travels between the nineteenth and twenty-first centuries, murdering people. To be fair, she does usually clean up after herself.

Liz's reimaginings of Sherlock Holmes, her Pippa Parker cozy mystery series, the Caster & Fleet Victorian mystery series (with Paula Harmon), the Magical Bookshop series, and the Maisie Frobisher Mysteries are available in ebook and paperback.

Liz lives in Cheshire with her husband and two sons, and when she's not writing or child-wrangling you can usually find her reading, messing about on

Twitter, or cooing over stuff in museums and art galleries. That's her story, anyway, and she's sticking to it.

Website/blog: http://lizhedgecock.wordpress.com
Facebook: http://www.facebook.com/
lizhedgecockwrites
Twitter: http://twitter.com/lizhedgecock
Goodreads: https://www.goodreads.com/lizhedgecock

BOOKS BY LIZ HEDGECOCK

To check out my books, please visit my Amazon author page: http://author.to/LizH (global link). If you follow me there, you'll be notified when I release a new book.

The Magical Bookshop (6 novels)
An eccentric owner, a hostile cat, and a bookshop with a mind of its own. Can Jemma turn around the second-worst secondhand bookshop in London? And can she learn its secrets?

Pippa Parker Mysteries (6 novels)
Meet Pippa Parker: mum, amateur sleuth, and resident of a quaint English village called Much Gadding. And then the murders began…

Booker & Fitch Mysteries (3 novels, with Paula Harmon)
Jade Fitch hopes for a fresh start when she opens a new-age shop in a picturesque market town. Meanwhile, Fi Booker runs a floating bookshop as well as dealing with her teenage son. And as soon as they meet, it's murder…

Caster & Fleet Mysteries (6 novels, with Paula Harmon)
There's a new detective duo in Victorian London . . . and they're women! Meet Katherine and Connie, two young women who become partners in crime. Solving it, that is!

Mrs Hudson & Sherlock Holmes (3 novels)

Mrs Hudson is Sherlock Holmes's elderly landlady. Or is she? Find out her real story here.

Maisie Frobisher Mysteries (4 novels)

When Maisie Frobisher, a bored young Victorian socialite, goes travelling in search of adventure, she finds more than she could ever have dreamt of. Mystery, intrigue and a touch of romance.

The Spirit of the Law (2 novellas)

Meet a detective duo – a century apart! A modern-day police constable and a hundred-year-old ghost team up to solve the coldest of cases.

Sherlock & Jack (3 novellas)

Jack has been ducking and diving all her life. But when she meets the great detective Sherlock Holmes they form an unlikely partnership. And Jack discovers that she is more important than she ever realised…

Halloween Sherlock (3 novelettes)

Short dark tales of Sherlock Holmes and Dr Watson, perfect for a grim winter's night.

For children

A Christmas Carrot (with Zoe Harmon)
Perkins the Halloween Cat (with Lucy Shaw)
Rich Girl, Poor Girl (for 9-12 year olds)

Printed in Great Britain
by Amazon

43148650R00088